Summoners Saga
Brianna's Quest

Summoners Saga
Brianna's Quest

By Shannon Lee Miller

DEDICATION

I never know what to write for these things, so I am going to keep it short and sweet. First and foremost, I need to thank my baby daughter, Lorelei, for not spilling coffee on my laptop even though she had so many opportunities to do so while sitting on my lap while I wrote. And for being such an awesome kiddo with napping or watching Pokémon so I could write, or even sitting on my lap but not trying to mess with the keyboard or anything. For a baby under one year old, that's unheard of!

Second, I need to thank Eric Herriman and Krystal Lampman aka Blue Jacket Girl (yeah, don't think I wasn't going to plug THAT!) for taking the time out of their busy lives to be my beta readers! Eric is ALWAYS there whenever my mom and I needed to borrow his canopy for shows and has always quickly and enthusiastically read and provided honest feedback to several things I've sent him. It's always nerve-wracking for me to send something out into the world, but Eric has always made it painless and a positive experience for me. And Krystal has always supported my writing ever since we became friends and started playing DDR back when… I won't say when, the DDR reference ages us enough! You two are the best, THANK YOU!

Lastly, to my folks for feeding me on almost a nightly basis, which allows me to come home and either read through stuff or do some editing without being totally zapped. And for letting me bow out of spending time on our business together to focus on just writing here and there. Without all that time, this whole thing probably would have taken me a few more months to finish. Thanks, mom, for all the time and food, and for mom and dad for being both big fans and supporters!

Okay, I'm done, let's get to the novel already…

TABLE OF CONTENTS

CHAPTER 1

I can't. I have to work in the morning. A double shift, yeah. Then I'm driving out to my folk's place for Thanksgiving holiday."

I glanced around me, trying to spot the tell-tale glimmer of the light rack on a cop car waiting in a speed trap. Or the faint interior light as they worked on their paperwork while waiting for people like me, illegally holding a cellphone to my ear and driving. My medium length, dark brown hair fell loose around my face and hopefully hid the cell phone's light. I never text while driving, and I'm not usually a fan of answering the phone while driving either. I'm actually a very responsible person, especially considering the penalties for doing as much in New York state. But this was Mark.

Annoying Mark. Particularly clingy tonight Mark. The same Mark who texted that if I didn't answer the phone, he'd be stopping over at my place to check on me. And after the day I had at work, all I wanted to do was crash into bed, alone.

He missed me. He *always* missed me. And despite the late-November rain, cold with streets strewn with wet leaves, he wanted to come over to the small house I rented. Unless I answered his phone call, so he could spend the past ten minutes trying to talk me into skipping out on some much-needed sleep and head over to his place.

Mark believed the world revolved around him.

I sighed as quietly as I could so the phone wouldn't pick it up. I slowed the car down as the rain seemed to come down heavier. The weather sat on the cusp of freezing, and with all this rain, I already drove under the speed limit. I hoped the rain came down hard enough that it wouldn't create black ice on the roads. Still, the car slipped and fishtailed along the backroads of my hometown.

Mark babbled on about something. I wasn't listening. I focused on trying to get home without passing out from fatigue or sliding off the road and crashing into a tree or pole. I assumed he prattled on about the same stuff he had been for the past week. *Bri, we should move in together. Bri, we should do more together. Bri, you need to work a job that will allow you to spend more time with me. Bri, you need to stop working overtime, what about me?*

Blah blah blah. It didn't matter what I said or wanted. I just… hadn't figured out yet how to break it off with someone who I knew wouldn't take no for an answer.

I blinked a few times, trying to wake my drooping, tired eyes. I held the phone with my shoulder, driving with one hand and using the other to wipe grit out of my eyes.

Suddenly, a gust of wind pushed my small car. The rain formed a blinding sheet, and I couldn't see more than a dozen or so feet ahead of me. I glanced down at the speedometer. Thirty-five miles an hour. Any slower, I grumbled in my mind, and I would never get home tonight. "Mark, can I call you back? This rain is coming down harder."

"Bri you are always doing this. Always trying to avoid a conversation. Were you even listening to me?"

"Mark, please—"

I felt air rushing past my lips. A horrible animal sound filled my ears. Flashes of light blinded me. My head erupted in pain, sharp and throbbing.

I remembered being a child, riding my first roller-coaster. The violent, elated feeling as my body whipped from side to side, no true sense of direction. All control was lost, except to hold on. And I knew that's all I could do now, a death's grip on the steering wheel.

The worst pain came with the sudden, halting jolt to my left side. I tried to breathe, but no air made its way in. I panicked, trying to grab at my throat. That's when I realized I still gripped the wheel so tightly I thought my knuckles were crushed. Letting go, I blinked. Tears fell away, but the narrow world, lit by my headlights, appeared all wrong.

The torrent of rain sluiced away the clumps of mud and weeds, all sliding the wrong way. The single working headlight showed a world on its side, and in motion.

My lungs allowed me a single, painful breath as I stared ahead at... a person? My eyes tore themselves away, focusing on movement farther in the distance.

I've seen big snakes while visiting the local zoo. Twenty-foot giants coiled and lounged in their enclosures, seemingly dead. They always creeped me out, unreal. I was glad for the thick glass between them and myself. This, though, this... was not one of them. And I have a fear of snakes.

The beast slithered forward, raising its upper half towards the stormy night sky. It rose, illuminated to monstrous proportions in the remaining high beam. The creature towered over the smaller human figure and opened its maw. A horrid sound filled my car, drowning out my own terrified screams. A deep, rumbling hiss and snarl, all wrapped into one world-shattering sound.

The man snapped his attention towards me. Even from several yards away, his blue-gray eyes, like storming clouds, bore into mine. That hard glare, surprise and anger, frightened me more than the beast beyond him. Dark, wet, shoulder-length hair clung to his face and neck. I couldn't make out what he wore except the soaked, heavy cloak snapping in the wind, hiding any suggestion of his figure in its shifting shadows. My scream died as my mouth remained open.

With a speed that seemed impossible, the man rushed forward, towards the beast. His arms rose over his shoulder, hands clasping a huge sword. The world around me spun and throbbed. It was hard to focus on him. Powerful anger, tinged with fear, filled most of my mind, distracting me.

The giant snake-thing screeched and lunged.

Sudden, blinding pain squeezed my eyes shut. Strange sounds roared around me as the wind howled, the rain and sleet pounded against the car. More demanding and intense though was the pain. I think I touched my head. I knew I had to do something. A voice mumbled in the distance. Asking me something. A man's voice, frantic and muffled at the same time.

My eyes stayed shut. They probably wouldn't have opened even if I tried. I think I was speaking. I could feel movement coming from my own face. I couldn't understand my thoughts. Pain. Just so much pain…

Something warm grabbed my arm and tugged gently. Through the cracks of my blurry eyes, a face hovered. All I could make out were eyes. Clouds at the end of a stormy sky, cooling, promising gentle rains and relief from the sun's pain. So much pain…

I didn't want to leave the warmth and weighted security of my comforter. Yet something wasn't right.

Opening my eyes enough to see without worsening the headache, I looked around the room. Everything was sideways. My side table with my phone. Muddy clothes laying on the floor. The beam of sunlight spilling in from a carelessly closed curtain.

I jumped up from my bed and looked around again, blinking several times. Something happened. Yet all I could remember was…

The accident!

A violent pounding resumed in my head as acid and saliva filled my mouth. I winced. I remembered some, now. My forehead smashing against the steering wheel. The blinding pains. And then, the man and monster…

"There she is," I heard a quiet, but familiar voice say. My nose caught the whiff of something, and I grimaced.

"No food," I muttered, closing my eyes and shoving a pillow over my face.

"Sounds like a concussion," I heard Mark's voice say as he set something down. A few seconds later, he was beside me, sitting on the edge of the bed. The sudden shift in equilibrium made my head pound harder, my stomach threatening me with nausea.

His fingers touched my head and I winced. "No, please."

"It's okay, babe," he said quietly, lifting his fingers from the swelling. "I'm just trying to make you feel better. Anything I can get you?"

"Peace and quiet and sleep," I muttered.

"Do you remember what happened last night?"

I groaned. This was one of the main reasons I wanted to break up with him. Always talking. Always clingy. Ever since I started dating Mark, I never felt like I was alone with myself, not even in my own home. I was really regretting ever giving him a key to the rental house. "Car accident."

"You must have hit something! Your car was tipped over on its side, and it looked like it rolled a few times."

I didn't want to remember, but flashes appeared behind my eyes. Watching mud slide down the rain-soaked windows. Headlights shining too brightly into the stormy darkness. A man...

"A man?" I wondered out loud.

Mark's hand found my shoulder, massaging it gently. "A man?" he asked with a hint of tense curiosity. "Did you hit a man?"

"No," I murmured. Yet there was more.

A creature. Massive. Larger than anything I had ever seen. It screamed. I remembered the sound and winced. "No, there was... hey!"

I could hear the smile in Mark's voice. "Like I said, I'm just trying to make you feel better, hun."

"Then leave me alone," I said with a little more strength.

"Well, what if the police come? What should I say?"

"Huh?"

"Well, I was the one who brought you home. I heard the crash and screaming over the phone and went out to find you."

"You didn't take me to a hospital? Call an ambulance?"

"You were cold and wet," Mark replied. "You were laying outside of the car, unconscious, in the freezing rain. I figured I should bring you back home. You've got some bruises, a few cuts, but nothing major."

"I have a fucking concussion," I interrupted through clenched teeth. "You're supposed to get checked out if you have a concussion. That's how you end up with post traumatic brain—"

"If you still want to go to the hospital—"

"No, never mind," I muttered, burrowing my face deeper into my warm, soft pillow. "I'll just take some ibuprofen or something."

"Assuming you didn't hit a man, what should I tell the police? You hit a deer? I looked around, but I couldn't find any carcasses. Then again, I'm not sure how a deer could have—"

"It wasn't a deer. I... I don't think I hit anything. Something hit me. But it was massive."

"What did it look like?"

I growled into my pillow. "Mark, I just wanna rest."

5

"Why didn't you grab your phone when you crawled out of the car?" he said, changing the topic. "You could have called me for help. I was shouting for you."

I sighed. I guess he wasn't planning on leaving any time soon. Maybe the faster we got through his interrogation, the sooner he would leave me alone to rest. "I didn't crawl out. That man—"

"Man?" I heard the jealousy in his voice and felt a shift on the bed beside me. "What man? The one you thought you hit? What did he look like?"

"I dunno. Weird. Gray eyes that also seemed blue. A cape. And a…" I stopped. I was going to say, *and a sword,* but no way would anyone believe that. I wasn't even sure it was true, and not just an effect of the concussion.

Mark was silent for a moment. "And?" I remained quiet. "You saw a man, and all you can remember is that he had gray eyes and a cape? What else was there about him?"

I rolled over onto my stomach, and away from Mark. "Seriously, please go. I don't feel well, and I just want to sleep."

"I just want to take care of you," he replied, sounding hurt. "And be here to answer questions for you. I had your car towed, but I'm sure someone called the police by now, considering the shape it's in. It won't take them long to trace the car back to you, and then they will be here, wanting to ask questions—"

"Who the fuck cares!" I screamed. It tore pain across my entire head, stabbing me behind my eyes, but I couldn't stand it anymore. "I want you to leave me alone! I need to rest!"

Mark sighed as he petted the part of my head that apparently wasn't hidden under the sheets. "Alright, baby. I'll leave you to get some more rest. Just don't forget, I will be out of town on business for a few days. I want you to call and text me several times a day, let me know you are okay and if you need anything."

"Fine," I replied, scooting away from his hand. I really didn't care for a moment if he was gone for a day or gone for a year. As long as he left me alone so I could have some peace and quiet as my brain pounded inside my skull. A few minutes later, I heard his truck start up in the driveway. I felt myself relax and before I knew it, I was asleep.

I turned my phone back on and looked at the time. 8:20 in the morning. I tried to remember what day it was. How long had I been sleeping? Squinting, I found the calendar app.

November 21st.

"Fuck," I said, getting up as fast as I could. Two days. I had been out for two days! I remember vaguely using the restroom and having a handful of crackers and some water to chase the handfuls of ibuprofen.

Two days.

My phone began to buzz and vibrate angrily. Missed calls. Unanswered texts.

Groaning, I flopped back onto the bed. I pondered calling work first, tell them what happened, that I would need another day off...

The first set of texts were from the boss. The last read, "You're fired. Please drop off your key at your earliest convenience."

"Well, fuck that," I mumbled, skimming the dozens of texts from Mark. Several asked how I felt, then why I wasn't answering. They grew from concerned to aggressive, asking where I was, what happened, to please call. I felt hollow, but I couldn't deal with him at the moment. Dozens of other texts. A few from the folks asking how the weekend was going. A few from coworkers who had my number.

And of course, the numerous missed calls and voicemails from Mark.

Any other girl would have been flattered someone cared as much about them. I received more calls and texts from Mark than everyone else combined. I should have cared that he cared so much and was worried about me, right? So then why did everything about him, when he wasn't around, made me feel off, like something was wrong?

I couldn't even bring myself to listen to the voicemails. I got up slowly, throwing some clothes on that weren't muddy but had been laying on the floor.

I didn't feel great, but I also knew I needed to talk to someone. In person. Get out of the house, maybe go find out how wrecked the car was.

There was one friend I always felt comfortable talking to, no matter how crazy something sounded. One friend who was always there to lend an ear, a ride, or whatever.

CHAPTER 2

D amn, that sucks about your car."
I blew a raspberry and took three more ibuprofen, dry.
"Are you sure you don't wanna see a doctor about that headache and goose egg?"

"Nah, it's fine," I replied, staring at the world passing by at sixty miles an hour, fighting the nausea already halfway up my throat. "I already don't have a job and need a new car. Don't want to add another fucking expense to that list."

Without turning, I knew the expression Kara was wearing. Green eyes wide and moist with growing sadness under a hood of tight blonde curls. Her small, thin lips pursed tightly, trying to hold back her thoughts. The same look my super sensitive friend had for anyone or anything that was struggling. At the same time, she could never keep her mouth closed for long, which made her a great friend to have when you didn't feel like talking; she could speak for both of us. Or a room full of people. I actually managed a small smile, the first in a few days, knowing those lips would open in three, two, one…

"You're too smart for that stupid job anyway," she blurted. "Way too good for this stupid hick town. I mean, I would miss you, but what—"

"Hell no," I replied, rolling my eyes as I turned to her. "No way I'm moving in with my folks."

"Yeah but, what about your little sister? You've barely seen her since your family moved."

I winced. I was really close to my sister, Elizabeth. I definitely missed her dearly. She was a few years younger than me, a senior in high school. But I was also her role model. I was old enough to drink. Now. I had my hookups for edibles which I used from time to time for my panic attacks. And when I was Elizabeth's age, I was drinking, or smoking, or popping gummies. I wanted my little sister to be better than me, while at the same time, I needed to be out on my own, doing my own thing. Feel like a responsible adult. Because that was the problem. When I still lived at home, we did everything together. We were inseparable. She would emulate me, trying to be older than who she really was. "She's better off without me there. Focus on her studies. Hang out with kids her own age. Maybe she's got a boyfriend already. I mean, I'll see her for Thanksgiving, if I can figure out how to get down there now without a car."

"I mean, I'm not going anywhere if you wanna borrow my car? That is, as long as you don't hit any big snakes with it." I could hear the grin in her voice.

I winced, the nausea getting the better of me. I closed my eyes and pressed the heels of my hands against the lids as I took a long, deep breath.

"Hey, Bri, you okay?"

"No," I mumbled, swallowing an acrid lump. "I'm gunna fucking puke."

"Whoa, not in my car, please. Hold it a minute, I'm going to stop at the town park up here."

I started to nod my head, but the growing pain and nausea was too much. Eyes still closed, I felt the car slowing and turning. Deep breath in, slowly exhale out, trying to keep my promise that I wouldn't cover the interior of Kara's car in puke.

Hearing the car shift into park, I didn't wait for her to turn the engine off before unbuckling my seat belt and flinging the door open. Cool November air hit me like a wall after the heat inside the vehicle, easing the nausea. Grabbing ahold of my purse, I climbed out, a little shaky, and walked over towards a pair of benches by the playground.

I practically grew up at this park, as did nearly everyone else who grew up in this town. Most of the park was a wide-open field, bordered on two sides by the woods, another by the main road for town, and the last by a large, flat cornfield with another, busier road in the distance. It was really your typical, small town park. Within the park stood several copse of pines, two baseball fields surrounded by soccer fields and kickboards, the playground on one side next to the rec hall, and behind us the small brick public bathrooms.

By the time I plopped down on the bench, the burning, water-in-the-mouth feel of looming nausea had subsided. Kara sat beside me, zipping her keys in her purse before setting it between us. For a few minutes, we sat in the sun and watched as three women either pushed kids on a swing or watched the rest as they ran around, squealing, racing up and down the slide. A pair of teens farther out on the soccer field kicked a ball back and forth, tossing up mud and wet sod with almost every pass. I really wanted to go for a walk. My muscles ached from laying around for two days. But my head pounded too much, and I worried the nausea would come back if I moved.

"A giant snake, huh?"

"Yeah," I replied, gingerly shaking my head. "With wings."

"And a weird dude with a sword." Kara sat quiet for not even a moment before continuing. "I mean, have you even thought of the possibility that maybe the car hydroplaned off the road and you flipped it across a ditch? That maybe what you saw was really something you brain conjured up after the concussion? I mean, what did Mark think of all of this?"

"I, well, I didn't quite tell him... everything," I replied, my eyes watching first the moms and kids, then the guys kicking the ball.

"Bri! Why are you hiding stuff from him? He even said he was worried and came out to get you. I mean, you're lucky. I wish I had a boyfriend that always wanted to be with me and do things for me. And save me from a crash."

"Hmm, it's not as great as it sounds."

"Uh oh, I know where this is going." Out of the corner of my eye, Kara shook her head as she tightened the scarf around her neck. "Bri, you can't be suspicious of every guy you date. No one is perfect. Not to be mean but you have your faults too, ya know?"

"Yeah, trust me, I know I'm not perfect," I replied. "And, yes, I know I have a bad track record with guys, but there's just something different about Mark."

"Is it because he's older?"

I paused a moment. Older? He did look a bit older than me, but not by much. I tried to think if he had ever mentioned how old he was. Maybe it was the concussion. I couldn't remember if he had ever mentioned his age. "No, it's not that. It's just... something feels off. I can't describe it.

Everything feels right when he's around, but then when I have time to myself, I realize I don't want to be with him."

"What about him seems off?"

"Like I said, I don't know. I can't describe it." I rubbed my hands together, partially to warm them, partially because I was starting to get anxious, frustrated. The nausea was returning. Closing my eyes, all I could feel was the throbbing pain, acid burning my throat while my hands froze. I just wanted to feel better. I just wanted to be free. "I don't really want to talk about it."

"Bri," Kara started, putting one of her cold hands over mine. "If anything is going on that shouldn't be, like, ya know, if he's hurting you or anything—"

"What?" I yelped. "No! Its, its nothing like that, trust me. It's just..." I suddenly felt dizzy, overwhelmed.

Trapped.

I pulled my hands out from under hers and stood.

Trapped. In pain.

The ground seemed to shift under my feet. Kara must have noticed. Jumping up, she grabbed me, holding me in a hug. "I'm worried about you, Bri. You shouldn't feel this sick, this dizzy. Lemme take you to the doctors."

"No, I'm fine. Just... just don't worry about it."

Kara gave a somewhat reserved smile. "Okay, Bri. I'll trust you for now if you say everything is all right. Just, you know, you can tell me anything."

I smiled back at Bri as I pulled away from her arms. "Thanks. You know, you really are my—"

The ground shook around us. Sod and rocks rained upwards. One of the kids fell off the swing as mothers and children screamed. Kara grabbed my arm, crying out as grass and mud both fell and rose around us. Still weak, I fell back against her, clumsily knocking the both of us over.

Something massive erupted from the ground a few feet from us. A hailstorm of pebbles and earth pelted our heads.

"What the hell is going on?" Kara cried out, gripping me tighter. I swear, if she squeezed any harder, she was going to shatter the bones in my arm.

11

I blinked some of the soil away, using my free arm as a shield so I could see. And what I saw made my heart stop.

Even though it had been dark out the night of the crash, there was no mistaking the massive body of the serpentine monster that rose from the ground, easily a hundred feet long. Long like a snake, except bigger than any I had ever read about or seen on television. It was a dark gray with dull, yellow markings along its sides and head. The head stared down at the screaming kids, its open maw wide enough to swallow a cow whole. What set it apart from any snake were the two, massive leather wings, like those of a bat, it unfurled as it rose above us, blocking out the sun.

Kara bawled, trying to stumble to her feet. I too attempted to stand, but Kara's efforts kept dragging me down. "Kara, please, help me!"

"Oh my god, I don't want to die, I don't want to die! Help! Help!" she continued to shout. With a final pull of my arm, she made it to her feet and half ran, half fell away.

The massive beast's head turned towards her.

"Kara, no! Stop!"

Kara faltered and looked back. I know I said stop. But I hadn't meant for her to stop. I really meant for her to wait and help me.

The remainder of the beast's body shot out from the hole like a bullet from a gun. Part of its body slammed against me hard enough to knock me to my hands and knees in the mud. I heard a scream. By some small miracle, the snake thing's body blocked me from seeing what silenced my best friend's scream.

I felt paralyzed. Frozen hands and knees stayed buried into the lose ground. Burning tears streamed down my face. My breath stuck in my throat, heart beating so wildly in my chest, I expected to fall dead of a heart attack.

The world around me seemed slow. I could hear screaming and a hissing, like one continuous sound. The beast's body still blocked the sun, cloaking me in its shadow. Nothing seemed to move. The horror didn't change. My hands in the mud could feel the ground warm and charged. Something solid, like a large stick, grazed my fingertips. It seemed to rise up itself into my hands. Unconsciously, my fingers wrapped around it.

I didn't want to die. I didn't want to die! Already, I couldn't believe Kara was gone. My head spun, and my body felt as if I had just survived yet another car accident.

With a cry, I pulled my hands out of the earth and sat up on my knees. My fingers gripped the massive stick as if my life depended on it. Underneath the mud, marks and exotic symbols were carved into the ancient, but smooth-worn rod. One end was adorned with bizarre objects, each hanging from pieces of thin, old fashioned rope and strips of stained cloth.

I looked past the staff. The beast had moved past me, coiling, and rising once again. It flared its wings open several times as if stretching. Large, gold, and black eyes bore down on me.

"No!" I screamed, raising the staff before me.

The snake thing's attention suddenly shifted, one eye looking up into the sky above. My own eyes followed.

A colossal, winged creature hovered above the park. I didn't even see where it had come from. It had to be the size of an elephant with three heads and three sets of wings atop a massive torso.

Gray feathers covered the torso, thick like an owl. Each feather, even from this distance, appeared to be edged with gold, silver, or black, giving this new creature a laced appearance. Sitting squarely above the torso, a head of black, eyes as round and dark as a crow, glared down at me. A wicked looking eagle's beak of black protruded from its face, sharply curved with lethal intent. Rising behind it I could see two massive black wings, almost encompassing the entire bird-thing.

But that was not all. To the left of the torso, where I guess a bird's shoulder would be if they had one, rose a silver-feathered head. Soft blue irises surrounded black pupils. Its light gray beak, thick and short, but pointed like an owl, would have been its most prominent feature if not for the tall crest of feathers it made rise and fall. To the left of the creature's torso, one atop the other, were two wings of the same glistening silver as the head. To the right of the black head rose a third of brilliant gold, as bright and shining as a statue of gold. Its black pupils were surrounded by a darker gold iris. Its yellow-gold beak was similar to that of the black head except its dangerous beak appeared more regal. This head had what looked like a mohawk of golden feathers, all the edges lined with a rose gold color. Similar to the silver wings of the left side, two golden wings were extended, one atop another.

"Ascalon," a voice spoke behind me.

13

I looked back, stunned to see the same man from the night before. His sword tip buried into the ground; his hands folded reverently on the top. His head was slightly bowed, and his lips moved quickly with words I couldn't hear. His eyes though, were opened and staring at me. Wide, blue-gray eyes, glistened in awe, as an incredible amount of white showed his fear.

All three beaks opened, an unworldly sound resonating in my head. I felt a desire to kill. To strike with revenge. A pure sense of something else, a burning need, but I couldn't understand what for.

My attention snapped back, focusing on the unearthly creatures. The one above me felt concerned, dangerous, but how I knew this I don't know. The silver head looked down at me while the other two turned to glare at the snake thing. Their beaks opened, hissing, and screaming as their short, thick tongues wagged. I climbed to my feet, an odd sense of calm rushing over me. The silver head turned, looking at the strange beast with its companion heads.

"Stand back!" I heard the man behind me shout.

Tension and pressure from strange thoughts and feelings filled my head. I looked to the snake beast and felt extreme fear, panic. I wanted to run. I could still feel the aches and bruises from the crash. But at the same time, a fearless calm struck me. Then anger. Seething rage. I wanted to run, hide, cry, terrified that I would end up like Kara. I also felt compelled to strike. I wanted to go after it, feel its flesh tear, hot blood spilling to the ground, filling my mouth.

With a howl of anguish, I raced towards it, both hands still clenching the staff. "Kara!"

Buffeted by the down stroke of the winged beast, it dove over me, its target the snake creature. With three terrible and separate cries, is enormous razor-like talons opened and struck at the snake.

Sharp pain, strange emotions, washed over me, leaving me feeling sick. The onslaught caught me off-guard. Collapsing to my knees, bile spewed from my mouth. I physically couldn't deal with wave after wave of what I now felt. I trembled, still puking, my hands white from gripping the staff. I could taste blood, but I knew I wasn't bleeding. I could feel flesh, my flesh, but it wasn't. Shredding. The pain reached an intensity I've never felt before. I rolled to my side, curled up, and screamed.

A hand gripped my shoulder. I could see the strange man beside me through blurry eyes. His oppressive presence silenced my scream, though I was in no less pain. Reaching up, I grabbed his wrist. "Please," I whimpered, trembling, suffering. "Help me."

His blue-gray eyes stared down at me, studying me. I could still hear, feel the battle raging. It seemed so foreign. Miles away. Yet I could feel it inside of me, as if they somehow fit inside of me. All that mattered, all I cared about, was for this man to help me. Again.

Gone was his cloak from the night before. Instead, he stood in front of me like a cosplayer from a renaissance festival. In the daylight, I could make out his costume, his form. Everything well-worn and stained. Almost black leather boots, stained with wear, reached to just below his knees. Dark brown leather pants had been tucked into the boots. A separate piece of leather armor encircled his waist, woven in numerous strips. Flattened, aged metal rings had been braided into the belt. Above encircled a long, wide belt of thick, unadorned leather. A sheath for his long sword hung from the belt, though he clutched the sword in his hand. An almost black hide made up his long-sleeved shirt. Over this he wore a thick vest of leather, woven in diagonal lines that met down the middle. Studs and rings embellished the strips. Everything he wore seemed battered, yet he still gave off a regal and powerful aura.

My eyes wandered to his chestnut hair that touched his shoulders. It wasn't exactly curled, but I could make out waves and rings in the locks. His lightly tanned face was unblemished, angular, and solid like cut granite. There was no emotion to his gaze, making me feel even more small and insignificant.

In that moment, I knew he was real. The crash had been real. Which meant...

I pleaded with him silently, trying to return his gaze with my own of desperation.

Something flickered in his face, as if he could read my thoughts.

"Please," I managed to croak. It couldn't have been more than a whisper.

Lowering himself, he wedged his shoulder under one of my arms. He yanked me to my feet without effort. I could barely stand. Struggling, I used the staff as a crutch as he held me up. "You did not tell me you were a Summoner."

"What?"

I could feel his head turn as he hurried me away from the nightmarish battlefield. That's when I noticed his breath. A warm, rich smell like fall spices. "You are a Summoner." He glanced at the staff I held with my left hand for balance.

"N-no, I'm not, I... I found it in the ground," I managed through clenched teeth. "A moment ago."

The man shook his head and grunted, guiding me behind the rec building. "Do not lose that staff," he ordered. "Do not let any harm come to it. Guard it with your life." One of the trinkets, a bit of old steel with a foreign word in symbols caught his eye. He touched it almost hesitantly. "Ascalon."

"What are they," I asked, nodding to the sky on the other side of the rec building. The snake thing had reached upward, trying to snatch the bird thing. For having wings, the snake-thing hadn't yet tried to fly. Darkness swam across my eyes. I didn't think I was going to be conscious much longer. "Why are they here, why is this happening to me?"

The man stood. He stared at me a moment before running off, leaving me weak and huddled against the building. I clutched the staff tighter. Like it would really protect me if either of those two creatures came for me. I closed my eyes, hoping that would make me feel better. It didn't. I could see Kara running, then the beast blocking my view of her death. I could still feel pains. Suddenly, something icy hot bit into my side.

I think I screamed. I heard it more than felt the tearing in my throat as darkness once again overwhelmed me.

CHAPTER 3

Once again, I woke up in my bedroom. My eyes cracked open and I stretched. Closing my eyes a moment longer, the late fall sun spread across the comforter, warming me. When I began to go from comfy warm to too hot, I threw back the comforter and opened my eyes.

"What the fuck!" Still holding onto the edge of the bedding, I pulled it back up to my chin.

Next to me leaning against the wall was the staff. I had forgotten about it. Next to it stood my nightstand with a glass of water. I couldn't remember getting a glass of water, so I assumed he did it.

The strange man sat across the room next to my door in a highbacked chair he must have brought from the kitchen. He looked disheveled and soiled, yet he sat calmly, his clean sword out and leaning against the wall beside him.

He narrowed those strange eyes at me. "Please, do not swear."

"Who the hell—"

His eyes narrowed as even more muscles in his face tightened. "Please—"

"Okay, fine," I said, realizing I was getting more irritated by his verbal purity than the fear and indecency I should have been feeling with this strange, armed man in my room. "Why are you in my room?"

He nodded once, slowly. "I promised to answer whatever questions you may have that I have the authority to give. However, I would ask that the favor be returned in kind as I have some of my own." He spoke in a low, rich voice, but not so deep as to be overbearing. His calm and careful intelligence made me feel as if he were older and wiser than how he appeared.

"Okay, fine, whatever."

"My name is Edrick."

"Last name?"

The man sat forward, resting his forearms on his thighs. "I do not have one. Where I am from—when I am from — it was common to address oneself by their given name and the place they hailed from. Last names did not catch on for over a century more. Now, what is your name?"

"What, what do you mean by… how old are you?"

"Answer my question first, Summoner."

"All right then, my name is Brianna MacArthur. And I'm not a Summoner." I paused a second. "And I would like you out of my apartment, please."

Edrick shook his head. "I am sorry."

"What? Sorry that you won't leave?"

"Both. I am sorry because you are a Summoner. The staff and your summon yesterday proves it," he said, nodding towards the staff still leaning near me. "And I am sorry because I cannot leave you alone. It is my duty to guard you now."

"Guard me from what? Those…things? That keep attacking me? Why is all this happening?"

He opened his mouth to speak.

"Wait. And who is making you protect me?" I felt a flush of anger rise into my cheeks. "Mark. Mark made you follow me, didn't he?"

"Mark?" Edrick frowned slightly. "I do not know anyone by the name of Mark. At least, not one that would still be alive."

"What do you mean any that would still be alive?"

"I believe you have asked several questions of me now," Edrick interrupted. "It is my turn again." He leaned back for a moment before speaking, crossing his arms. "You claim you are not a Summoner. However, you withdrew the sacred staff from the Chaos Realm and used it to summon the most powerful and dangerous creature from that place."

"I-I couldn't have done that." I shook my head. "I don't know what is going on. I don't understand any of this. Besides, why would I cause a car accident that nearly killed me?"

Edrick narrowed his eyes, staring deep into me again. "No, not the wivre. I have been tracking him for a while now in my search for the Lyndheart. No, I was speaking of the summon from yesterday. Ascalon."

I moaned heavily, falling back into the nest of pillows behind me, and pulling the comforter up over my head. It was honestly too warm to be laying under such a thick blanket, but the darkness and feeling that I was being protected, cocooned, was worth it.

"Brianna, I have not asked my question."

"Go away!" I shouted. "Just leave already!"

"I already told you. Dragon's wivre is after you for some reason, and I know it has also been tracking down the Lyndheart here in the New World. Somehow, you are connected with all of this."

"No, I'm not!" I shouted, realizing too late what a child I must have sounded like. "If you don't leave, I am going to call the cops."

"I can see you are still too overwhelmed by everything that is going on," he said. I could hear the creak of the chair. He must have stood up. I also heard another strange sound I didn't recognize. "I will go out into the kitchen and make us something to drink. Rest some more if that is what you need. Come see me when you are ready."

I heard him walking out of the bedroom, although he left the door open. It didn't matter. I wasn't planning on getting out of bed.

For what seemed like a long time but was probably only a few minutes, I stayed hidden under my blanket cocoon. Yet all the warmth and darkness brought me were more memories. Feelings. The echoes of the words the man Edrick had just spoken. Kara's death. Pain. Power. A panic attack began crushing my chest. I tried to take deep breaths, knowing if I didn't get it to stop now, it was only going to get worse. I had to stop thinking.

With a snarl, I threw the blanket back. I was still in a light sweater and jeans. Both though were soiled, and all I could think about was how now I would have to wash all of my bedding before the day was done. Trying to shake the thoughts and panic from my mind, I walked across the room. Closing the door loudly with a kick of my foot, I ripped open my drawers and pulled out some clean clothes. I ran a brush through my hair after a quick two-minute shower and checked all of my bruises and cuts. I frowned. They were gone. I put a hand to my head, suddenly realizing that the headache I had been feeling for days now, the lethargy and aches… they were all gone. Don't get me wrong, I was grateful. Yet it was really, really odd.

Any odder than everything else that has been happening to you lately?

I looked around for my purse but couldn't see it anywhere. Edrick must have placed it elsewhere.

No. Probably not, I realized with a sigh. I had left it on the bench. I didn't recall grabbing it while I was running and trying to save my ass from that beast thing. What had that man called it? Wivre? And what about the other one?

How did he even know what it was called? How could he act so casual about it?

I threw open the door, walking past the staff next to my nightstand. Something reached out towards me, a feeling. My hand went to grab it, but I forced my hands into my pockets. I didn't want anything more to do with whatever was going on. And that staff was definitely involved.

"Okay," I said, making my appearance into the kitchen. "I'm up. I'm all healed, somehow." I noticed Edrick helped himself at the kitchen table. In front of him sat a petite porcelain cup wrapped in delicately painted flowers and a decorative web of golden colored metal. A strange metallic container with a long handle of the same gold-like metal as the cup sat on the gas range behind him. He blew across the top of the small cup before taking a sip. It smelled strong, spicy. A rich coffee scent, but earthy and nutty. "And I see you have had some time to enjoy your... whatever that is. Time for you to go now."

Edrick smiled softly. "This has not been the first time I have had to deal with doubt and criticism towards me and my order, and the events that go unnoticed to most men their entire lives." He pulled another of the small porcelain cups from out of his satchel. Reaching to the long-handled container, he carefully poured the dark, steaming liquid into the second cup. "Here," he said, pushing it carefully in my direction. "This will help."

Keeping a wary eye on him, I moved toward the counter to the right of the range. With an angry stab of my finger, I turned on the Keurig, listening to the hissing and popping as water quickly began to heat up. Without so much as blinking, I continued to stare at him as I dropped a pod into the machine, grabbed an empty cup from the cupboard, and pushed another button to fill the cup.

Edrick's smile grew wryer as he watched me grab my full cup and move to the far side of the small, square table, which, really wasn't that far away, maybe an arm's length, before sitting down.

"Not a tea drinker," I muttered, burying my nose into the aromatic steam wafting up from my mug. "And I don't drink tea from strange guys."

Edrick nodded once, grinning and sipping again from his petite cup. "It is not tea."

We sat that way for several minutes, each sipping our drink of choice, studying each other. I wondered for a bit what was going through his mind. Did he honestly believe the fantasies he was spewing? It all seemed something a crazy person would say. Especially someone with a long freaking sword. But at the same time, he had been nothing but polite. He had more than enough chances to hurt me, hell, even kill me. Or at the very least, rob me. Instead, he was here claiming to protect me. And nothing he had done up to this point convinced me that he didn't genuinely believe what he said. At the same time, I don't think I could really convince even myself that all of what he said was actually fantasy. Had I not been attacked by the same creature, twice, and been saved, twice, by Edrick? Didn't that strange, three-headed mutant bird hover over me yesterday? I could have sworn I was feeling what it felt, understood its thoughts to some degree.

I tipped the mug back once more, realizing with a pang of sadness that it was now empty.

Edrick seemed to notice as well, pushing his tiny cup off to the side a few inches. "Are you better now, Brianna?"

"Just… call me Bri," I muttered, debating whether to get up and grab a second cup or not. "And yeah. Sorry, but I'm a bit of a psycho bitch in the morning."

Edrick winced. "Please, the foul language."

I rolled my eyes. "Okay, what are you, some religious nut or something?" I dropped the mug heavily back onto the table. "Can't even say bitch in my own apartment," I muttered under my breath.

He sighed and looked down at the table. "I grew up in a time when cursing truly meant something. And saying the Lord's name in vain was a stain to the soul one could not easily clean."

"Okay, that is like, the third time you have made a reference to time," I said, really starting to get creeped out again. I began to wonder if maybe this man was more dangerous than he was letting on. Which made me panic. Now that I didn't have my purse or cell phone, and I didn't have a land line, should I make a run for it to the neighbor's house to call the cops? Tight bands of anxiety began to wrap their achy fingers around my chest and back. I forced myself to take a deep breath. Carefully, I asked, "How old are you, really?"

"Does my age make any difference to our situation?"

"Uh, first of all, there is no 'our situation'. But yeah, unless I start getting some real answers that make any sense, I'm not doing or saying anything more."

"I have not even mentioned anything in that regard."

"Here's the rundown. You found and saved me twice in a matter of days. Strange creatures are popping up when you are around. And then you bring me back to my home, and…" The realization hurt, squeezing the air from my lungs. "Wait, how did you even know where I lived?"

"I followed you the other night when that man brought you back here. I… wanted to make sure you were okay."

I shook my head. Even though I felt better, I also felt a headache coming on. "Okay, know what? This isn't going anywhere. Why don't you tell me exactly who you are and why you are here. Meanwhile, I'll decide whether or not to call the cops on you."

Edrick sighed, folding his hands together on the table. He took a moment to compose himself before beginning. "Alright, perhaps an explanation is in order. As I have said before, my name is simply Edrick. I am from an old town called Colchester in England. I do not know my family other than my father who took me to learn the way of the Guardians soon after I was born, in the year 903 of our Lord." I opened my mouth to say something, but he held up a hand and I shut it. "I think it would be best for us both if I finish my story first. Then, you may ask for clarification.

"I know little of Colchester. I was brought to the city of Nicomedia, or what has also been called Izmit in modern day Turkey, as an infant. There, I trained and was educated for nearly a hundred years until the Citadel was moved to the city of Ani in Armenia. In that city, known then as the city of A-Thousand-And-One-Churches, we built several of our own to house and train our growing ranks. It was also an ideal, centralized location for Guardians to travel to when necessary as it allowed us to journey easily to any part of the known world.

"In the year 1101, soon after I had completed my studies, the first crusade had begun. Several of us were sent to aid the Byzantine forces in establishing safe pilgrimage routes for Christians." Edrick rubbed his knuckles thoughtfully. "The Guardians were established thousands of years earlier to protect men from those of the Chaos Realm. Yet during the time of the Crusades, our fascination with Christianity and our true mission became rather blurred. We fought alongside Christians for the next few hundred years. Our numbers dwindled as many were killed. Guardian youths that were not of Christian mothers and fathers were not accepted into the Citadel. Many Guardians gave up the... right to couple, entirely, adding to the depletion of our numbers. When I first joined the order, there were thousands of us protecting men and Earth. Only one hundred and ninety-three of us currently remain."

I could feel myself trembling slightly, even though the mid-morning sun was blazing through the window, making my back feel rather on the warm side. The way this man spoke was intimate. I could see it in his face, in his eyes. Yet… how could any of this be even remotely possible?

Edrick looked back up, blinking, his eyes focusing on me as if he had forgotten he was speaking to someone else in the room. "When the Inquisitions began, many Guardians gave up their ancient ways and lived out their lives as mortal men. We were targeted for our powers, which seemed to them as powers of the devil. Others, like myself, went into hiding. For hundreds of years now, we have grown used to being on our own, hiding in the shadows of civilizations. For a while, many of us began to think our mission had come close to completion. That is, until recently.

"Our mission as Guardians, as I said before, is to protect men and Earth from those of the Chaos Realm. It is a place beyond ours. In the past, there were men who had inside them the ability to warp and tear the fabric of the universes. This allowed our closest neighbor, the Chaos, to be exposed to our own, and visa verse. Over the millennia, many humans have been sucked into that other place. We have no idea what it is like, as none has ever returned to tell. I personally do not believe any lived long, if what has come out is any indication of what awaited them. Many mysteries man has described as monsters, fantasy creatures, the supernatural… most of these things are real. These beings have made their way here since the dawn of man. The same spark that gave man sentience is what weakens the barriers between the two realms.

"For thousands of years, the only ones who have been able to control these breaks in the realm, from creatures flooding the planet, have been the Guardians. In the distant past however, these tears and breaks were much more common. People with power beyond their understanding, the Summoners, used them without understanding its effects on this world and on humankind. Once the Summoners were controlled and then eliminated, Guardians were able to restore some order and balance. We have spent the past few hundred years trying to repair the damage the Summoners have done. We dismembered the great fiend who escaped into our realm to claim it as part of the Chaos Realm, the Lyndwyrm. Dragon and his ilk have been trying to recover all the parts in hopes of resurrecting him.

"During the Crusades and Inquisition, our efforts waned, and they were able to accomplish just that, minus the piece that will bring all his parts to life, the Lyndheart. There have been no signs of it for hundreds of years in the Old World, and I began to suspect several years ago that perhaps it had been hidden in the New World. And then I caught wind that minions of the Chaos Realm had grown more active around this place, this New York. I was tracking the wivre when it attacked you the other night. Then, to my surprise, you revealed yourself yesterday to be a Summoner. And female! Two things which should have been impossible, and yet you also showed your powers by summoning the most dangerous creature from the realm, one in which even the Lyndwyrm had been trying to escape — Ascalon."

He shook his head, his eyes boring hard into me. "It is no coincidence these things are happening. You are important enough for them to want to kill. Which means you are important enough for me to need to protect you until I can find out why exactly. At the same time, with the state of the Guardian order, we cannot have Summoners rising once again. And the fact that you are a girl—"

"Woman," I corrected. "Eighteen was a few years ago for me."

Edrick scoffed and smirked. "Female. It is impossible. I would not believe it myself had I not seen the staff in your hands and God's own weapon in the sky."

"So, you mean, all these Guardians and Summoners you've been babbling on about have all been males?"

"That has been the way of things since the dawn of mankind. And before you ask, we do not understand why. In the past, religious reasons were accepted. The various differences between men and women have also been cited. Yet none have proven to be the absolute reason. It has simply always been that way. Until you."

24

I slouched in my chair, letting out a deep breath as I crossed my arms. "Well, I mean, that was a great story and all. But maybe now it's time for you to go." I felt the chills run down my arm again. "I… I need to go find my purse, and my phone. I need to call my friend's parents. I need to make some calls about a new car, job. I need to call my—" I was about to say 'boyfriend', but was he? He hadn't shown up at all today, or last night. Was he even back yet from his work trip? Maybe he had tried calling me, but without being able to check my cell, who knew?

"That is fine. I will accompany you."

"Ah, no. I'm going to do what I gotta do to get some normalcy back into my life. You can go and check yourself back into whatever rehab, conspiracy theory cave you came out of. Oh, and take that weird staff as well."

Edrick narrowed his eyes as his lips tightened. I was worried about what he was thinking until he stood up from the table and nodded to me. "Very well. If you truly are not a Summoner, then you shall never see me again." He grinned, leaning over the table slightly. "Though I have a feeling you will see me again in due time." He opened up a satchel he had with him. Dumping out the remnants of the strange pot on the stove and the small cup I was offered, he wrapped them in a thick cloth and put them away. I watched him, unnerved, as I stood up by the door.

"Let's hope not," I grumbled, opening the door for him.

Edrick went into my bedroom, returning quickly with the staff in one hand. I shuddered as he brushed past me, the staff bumping my arm. "No one can tell what the future holds. Especially not a Summoner."

Without a word, I slammed the door shut behind him, locked it, and turned the deadbolt. Through the window, I watched him turn and look back a moment before shaking his head and walking off. I didn't stop watching until he had rounded the bend further down on the road and was no longer visible.

Feeling the gravity of all the events of the past week falling down around me, I sat at the kitchen table. As the panic elephant sat on my chest, trying to crush the air from my lungs, I began to cry.

25

CHAPTER 4

After some consideration, I was grateful that I didn't have access to a cell phone. I couldn't imagine the number of calls and texts I would be getting right about now. I still got a lot of instant messages online, as well as a few emails. I ignored them all, except the one from Mark. *I'm going to be out of town for a few more days on business,* it read, and it was time stamped before the events of Kara's death and the latest attack. *When I get back, we need to talk.*

A shudder went through me as I closed the lid to my laptop. I hadn't done much in the past few hours except cry and go online and look through sites mindlessly. No matter what I did, I couldn't seem to get Edrick out of my mind. I didn't want to think of him, of the stories he told. It made me think of the accident. Of Kara. It made me think of Mark and that made me feel sick to my stomach and made my anxiety rise. After staring at the closed lid a moment, I forced my gaze to move around my bedroom. I spotted my bed. The sheets and comforter were pulled back into a wrinkled wad. Dirt and dried mud soiled the bottom sheets. I sighed. I hated doing laundry, but it would be something to do. Something to keep my mind off of things. And that way, I could always borrow someone's cell phone and call into work and try to get my job back. After everything that had happened the past week, I was going to need money, and something to take my mind off things.

Time passed in a strange way, and I didn't remember everything that happened. I gathered a large basket of clothes and sheets and a handful of whatever change I could find lying around. As fast as I could to get out of the cold drizzle, I hiked the mile down to the laundromat. Not a lot of people were there, which was just as well. I didn't feel much like talking to anyone. One young mom, with two kids crawling all over her while she was trying to fold clothes, let me borrow her phone. I tried to explain the events of the past few days to my boss, to get my job back, but actually hearing that I was fired from my irritated boss' mouth still stung. I sat and watched the clothes spin around and around, numb, trying not to cry. Now I was jobless, didn't have a car, a cell phone, and my purse with all my ID and cards and cash was gone. My best friend, Kara...

The feeling of a wide belt being squeezed tightly around my chest and back started to manifest. Fatigue. Anxiety.

Trying to take deep breaths, I looked out the window.

Something stared at me.

It was hard to tell if it was a man or a woman. Regardless, they were short. Was it a kid being creepy? They stood outside in the cold November drizzle, a black hood and cloak wrapped around them to where you couldn't see anything but the material. Yet somehow, as I stood and began to move toward the door, I knew they were looking at me.

As I reached the door, I wondered for a second if it was Edrick. But no, the figure stood too short. Stepping out of the laundromat and walking around the building, I couldn't see any sign of the hooded person. Not even a footprint in the November mud. Stupid me, I left my coat on the dryer, and now stood looking ridiculous shivering in the wintry drizzle. I hurried back into the warm safety of the laundromat, chilled by more than the weather. Was it someone Edrick had following me? Mark? Or was something else strange about to happen? Like I needed anything else in my life at the moment.

The buzzer on the dryer finally went off as I re-entered the laundromat. I shoved my sheets and everything into a garbage bag to protect them from the rain before putting it in the basket. All alone now, I shuddered, still feeling as if someone were watching me. Taking a few deep breaths and a quick glance around the sides of the building, I began the mile hike with a basket of blankets back home.

After locking the door behind me and forcing myself to do some chores, I had forgotten about the figure until I looked outside. Night came fast as it always did this time of year, around 4:45 in the afternoon. The darkness reminded me of the hooded figure. I tried to tell myself I wasn't being watched. No matter how hard I looked into the darkness, how much I told myself no one was there, I felt lately a pervasive presence. But, if I had to be honest with myself, it was more unnerving than threatening, which was why I first thought it was Edrick.

Edrick. I literally shook my head as if that would shake the thoughts from my mind. I needed to think of something else.

Food. I needed to eat.

I didn't have much in my apartment in the way of food. I no longer had a car to go shopping with. And I could have ordered food online, but I didn't have any cards or cash on me to pay it with. Instead, I kind of grazed on whatever odds and ends I could find. Some stale Oreos. Half a sleeve of old crackers. Some grapes that were closer to being raisins than grapes. I nibbled as I continued some light cleaning, keeping my body busy as that seemed to be the key to not thinking.

I entered my bedroom for the first time since coming home. Plopping into my still unmade bed, I let go a long breath, feeling my body unwind. My eyes passively took in the room. They settled on something I hadn't noticed before. The pile that did not belong to me. Literally on my dresser. Mark must have made a spot by pushing several knickknacks off to the side and left several pants and sweaters and shirts on it. On top sat a small travel toiletry bag. I groaned. I forgot he had brought me back home the other day. He must have also brought some of his things over, thinking he was going to stay, that I would want my hero staying over. Even though we had been dating several months, the electric attraction I had felt for him in the beginning had totally died. Now, he was nothing more than an annoying, almost intrusive guy who I really didn't want anything to do with anymore.

Seeing the pile of clothes one more time sparked an anger in me. Storming over to my laptop, I opened it up rather violently and got on the messenger app I shared with him. *Mark,* I began to type. *Look, I need to talk to you. I didn't want to do this over text, but—*

Everything went dark. I yelped and jumped as the electricity snapped off. Everything became that strange silence that exists when nothing electric works.

"What now?" I muttered, trying to calm my racing heartbeat. I sat in the dark a moment. I was sure I had a flashlight, but I hadn't used it in a long time. Groping my way and trying not to stub my toes on the way to the kitchen, I opened up a couple of the junk drawers, using my hand to rummage through them slowly. When I felt something that felt like the handle of one, I clicked the button.

Nothing.

"Fuck," I swore. I was sure I didn't have a backup one as, well, that was my backup to electricity. Hopefully, it was only the circuit breaker. I had a rough idea of where it was in the small crawl-space cellar at the rear of the house. By now, my eyes were starting to adjust to the gloom. Grabbing a coat, I stepped outside and carefully began making my way around the house. At least the clouds had grown patchy enough to allow some scattered moonlight.

The growl came from all around me.

I had heard stories about people feeling like their insides froze. This was sort of the same thing, but it felt more like my insides had been dunked into a pool of ice water in the middle of a polar vortex. I had nothing on me, nothing with me or around me, I could use as a weapon. Panicking, I turned to head back into the house. At least inside, I would be—

Something monstrous stood at the door. Nearly as tall as myself, its head was lowered, and I could see a glint of moonlight in its yellow eyes. My mind reeled.

Something warm slid over my shoulder. I shrieked as a hand grabbed my arm, jerking me backwards. "Get behind me," I heard the hushed voice say slowly.

I fell behind the figure as he swept his way in front of me. That's when I caught the strange smell of spices. "Edrick," I whispered.

"Stay back, and do not run," he snarled. I could see him now, step by step advancing on the giant wolf. I say wolf but it was massive. Larger than any wolf I knew could possibly exist. Especially not in Upstate New York. Its shoulder rose as high as Edrick. A silvery white coat of thick, mangy fur covered the beast. Yellow stained teeth, several inches long, filled its maw as it wrinkled its muzzle into a snarl. Its large golden eyes locked hard on me, and I shivered, feeling it inside of me.

No, wait, I could feel myself in its steady gaze. The excitement of finding the prey. The growing fear of the man.

Edrick continued to advance on the beast. He held his large sword in both hands, steady. Along the length of the blade, I could see a faint, reddish glow of strange figures. It reminded me of ancient languages, runes. I was sure I hadn't seen them before when the sword was out.

The wolf snapped its muzzle at Edrick, advancing a few steps itself.

"Is it worth dying for?" Edrick said, moving his sword from side to side. "You would not be the first amaroq that has gotten in my way."

I could feel the change from excitement to hesitation. As if deciding it wasn't worth the fight, the wolf barked and snapped its mouth shut. I could feel its yellow eyes glare at me a moment before loping off into the woods across the street.

But that wasn't the only wolf to retreat into the night, from my mind. I don't know how many, exactly, but there were several.

A cold rain had begun to fall again as clouds moved in to cover the glow of the moon. Shivering despite the coat, I could feel tears forming in my eyes. "What the fuck is an am-ama-rock?"

Edrick stayed where he was a moment before sheathing his sword, turning to face me.

"Why is this happening to me?" I whispered, my teeth chattering.

"Come," he said, this time gently. He reached out and took my hand. Without another word, he guided me inside.

The inside of the house still sat in darkness. I stood by the kitchen table, still shivering under the weight of my now wet and cold winter coat. I could hear Edrick rummaging around the pack that had been slung across one shoulder. In less than a minute, I could hear him striking something, then a glow coming from a small oil lantern. He placed it on the table, turning a knob. It grew brighter as the flame grew larger. "You know why this is happening," he finally spoke, his gray-blue eyes boring into mine, "but you need to acknowledge it for yourself. I cannot force you."

He stood over me, intimidating. I shook my head. "No, I don't know what is going on. This has been a week from Hell. I'm losing everything. I'm being hunted. Everything is just—"

Gently, he pushed down on my shoulder, and I plopped heavily into the kitchen chair, my hand pressed tight against my chest. "Breathe," he continued to speak gently. "Slow, controlled breaths."

That's when I noticed I was nearly hyperventilating, my chest burning with the painful grip of an anxiety attack. I took a deep breath. Edrick moved to the chair across the table and slid gracefully into the seat. He folded his hands on the table in front of him. In the flickering lamp light, I could see his eyes, steady as a mountain, watching me. Waiting.

I stared back, captivated. I took another deep breath, trying to ease the pain in my chest and upper back. My week *had* been from Hell. I had no idea what was going on. Yet, every time my life had been threatened, Edrick had been there. A man who seemed to know so much yet didn't seem to be a part of this world. A man who faced any danger with a sword in his hands. A man who just this morning sat at my table, calmly sipping his weird coffee. How, amidst everything that was going on that should have been impossible, was he able to remain so calm, so cool, so collected?

"Better?"

I blinked, feeling drained, and tired, yet relaxed. I felt as if I had only been staring at him for a moment, breathing. I knew though it had been a lot longer. Minutes? An hour? I took another deep breath and let it out slowly as I nodded. Just then, the power clicked back on, blinding me for a moment.

Edrick reached over and took his lamp, blowing out the flame and setting it aside, waiting for it to cool.

"You must forgive me," he began softly, running a hand through his still damp, chestnut hair. "I forget that the world I am from and the world that most humans know of are two different places. I will try to remember this going forward, try to be more guiding and understanding of the situation you must be facing. Yet, I will be honest. I am surprised that until now, you have had no idea of what you are, of what you are capable of."

"What do you mean?" I asked. I felt so tired, all I wanted to do was sleep.

"Despite your protestations otherwise, you are a Summoner." He glanced over to his left, and I caught sight of the staff resting against my counter. I hadn't seen him carrying it, yet he must have. "Somehow, one of significant power as well. This staff is unique in that it holds relics from great Summoners and Guardians of the past." Reaching out, he brushed his fingers against the shard of glinting metal with characters I couldn't read across it. "You have summoned a creature from the Chaos Realm that would be difficult for a learned Summoner, and impossible for one with no training. I understand the shock and confusion you must be feeling. Your brain is trying to protect you by denying what seems the impossible.

31

But I am begging of you, Brianna. Unless you begin to embrace the idea of your new identity, things will only get worse, and there may come a time in which I cannot protect you. While I will help you as much as I can, give you guidance, I am also sworn to a duty that I must eventually continue.

"You, Brianna, are a Summoner. And the sooner you embrace this concept, the sooner I can assist in your training, and the safer you will be. But that is a decision which you need to make, which you must accept on your own terms. I can do nothing more than try to express to you the gravity of the situation you are in and the responsibility you must uptake if you are to survive what may come."

I hadn't meant to, but I was so tired, I rested first my arms on the table, then leaned my weight against them. By the time Edrick had finished talking, my forehead was pressed into my arms, and I could no longer keep my eyes open. A few tears slipped out. I felt beyond exhausted. Defeated. Like I had finally accepted, in a small way, that this was it now. Nothing was going to go back to the way it was as of last week. I took another deep breath. What would that mean for me?

CHAPTER 5

My eyes opened and I fully expected to still be seated at the table. Except I knew I wasn't. My head rested against my pillow, and I could feel myself snuggled deep under the clean blankets and comforter on my bed. I felt relaxed. Rested. As far as I could recall, I hadn't had a single dream. I laid in bed a few minutes, feeling better than I had in a week. All the stiffness and pains and stress I had been feeling had faded away. Not that I felt like I was bubbling with energy. Yet I was calm. Refreshed.

As I got up and changed into some clean clothes, I realized that I had fallen asleep at the table the night before. And my coat that should still be on was folded neatly on my desk chair. Which must mean Edrick had carried me in, took my coat off, and tucked me into bed, without waking me.

Edrick. I knew I shouldn't trust such a strange man with his wild tales. Yet there was something about him I was utterly drawn to. Even if I didn't believe almost anything that came out of his mouth, I could listen to him. His stories, his view of the world. I felt utterly safe when he was around, but that was because he had proven himself numerous times already that he wasn't a threat to me. Which meant he really was concerned about my welfare. About making sure I stayed unharmed.

Maybe, I suddenly found myself thinking as I pulled a thick sweater over my head, pulling it down to my waist, maybe I should give him a chance. Try to see what this training he wanted to do was all about. God knows I didn't want to get hurt, and who knew when there would be a time when Edrick wasn't around. And if these horrible things were going to keep happening to me, it wouldn't be fair to allow more innocent people, like Kara, to get hurt, killed.

Tying my hair into a ponytail and looking myself over once in the mirror with a nod, I stepped out of the bedroom and made my way to the kitchen.

Edrick sat at the table. I could tell he positioned himself so he could keep an eye out the window, and one eye on the doorway. From his vantage point he could see the small living room that lay between the bedroom and kitchen and the front of the house. Once more, he sat calmly, steam rising from the small, ornate cup of exotic coffee in front of him. He must have heard me get up. Across the table sat one of my mugs, filled with the aromatic goodness of a hot, black cup of coffee.

I slid into the chair, grabbed the hot mug in both hands and took a slow sip, savoring. That first sip of coffee in the morning was always my favorite.

"Thank you," I said, setting the mug back down.

Edrick smiled. I found myself blushing. "You are welcome," he replied, lifting his cup to his own lips and sipping.

We sat that way for probably fifteen minutes in silence. Occasionally glancing out of the kitchen window into the gray, drizzly world outside. Sipping our respective drinks. Now and then, I would pretend I didn't notice him looking at me, studying me. And then I would do the same, yet also knowing he knew I was watching him. The whole time it felt odd, strange, to be relaxed and sipping drinks with a total stranger in my kitchen. A stranger with a sword strapped to his waist and a huge, exotic looking staff leaning against the counter beside him.

Was he still just a stranger?

Unconcerned. Unthreatening. He almost felt like a reluctant friend at this point. Had he slept at all last night? If he didn't, I couldn't tell. Knowing what little I did so far about him, I assumed Edrick did sit up all night, most likely guarding me and keeping an eye out for whatever else decided to try to come up to the house.

When I had finished my coffee, I stood up and walked around the table to where Edrick sat. He watched me the entire way in silence. His eyes betrayed nothing as I reached out and hesitantly grabbed hold of the staff. It clinked softly as some of the baubles on it bumped against one another.

I studied it for a moment, realizing how strange it was to hold such a massive stick. How it felt like I had always held it, how familiar it felt.

"Okay," I finally spoke. "Let's start training, I suppose."

Edrick raised one eyebrow at me, though the tightness around the corner of his lips betrayed his excitement. "Are you sure, Brianna? Once we begin training, nothing will be the same again."

"It already isn't," I said quietly. With a final gulp, I drained my mug and placed it on the table with a thunk. "Yeah, let's do this."

The clouds began to wander as the morning sun shone, radiant and warm. It was still a little chilly out, and everything was soaked, but at least I was feeling better, and the day promised to improve. With a little help from me to navigate the kitchen, we made a quick breakfast of whatever was left in the apartment. After throwing our dishes in the sink, we stepped outside.

I leaned against the staff and watched him as he stood, facing the emerging sun for several minutes. Finally growing bored, I asked, "So, I thought you were going to train me?"

"I am," he hesitated. "I am trying to think… how." He turned, studying me from head to toe, as if looking for something. "You already have an innate ability to use the runic staff, yet you do not know how to use it consciously. The summon you have made thus far has been beyond my ability to handle.

"When a Guardian starts his training," he seemed to start over, "we spend nearly a hundred years learning what we can scholastically, as well as combat skills. How to handle various weapons, hand-to-hand. We study ancient wars and battles that have been documented throughout the ages to learn strategy. We learn games and mock fights so as to better formulate tactics in a split second."

"A hundred years?" I asked. "I don't think I plan on doing this for a hundred years. Most people don't even live that long." Kara's scream flashed through my head, forcing a chilled shudder racing along my skin. She died so suddenly, so easily. I was only—

"I know," he said, his voice snapping me back to the present. "Summoner training is not that much different, and entirely so, from what

I have read. The lesson I cannot teach is bridging the Chaos Realm to this one. To reach through the fabric of our reality, plucking specific beings and forcing them to appear here... I lack that skill, but since you have already done so, I may not have to try and teach you how to do this. That part you will have to figure out how to do on your own, on command."

Edrick began to pace the yard, one hand on his chin, the other playing with the hilt of his sword. "In your case, the most difficult part will be in both the summoning and control of the beasts. A few of my companions studied the ways of the Summoners to better understand their connection with the Chaos Realm. How it was explained to me was that Summoners could feel inside of the beasts."

My mind went back to a couple days ago when the large, three-headed bird thing appeared in the sky before me. I remember thinking, feeling, strange. Was this what Edrick was talking about? Was I feeling inside the mind of the creature?

No, I corrected myself. *Minds*. I was connected to all three minds. That would explain why I felt so sick. I couldn't really describe how it felt to feel inside the mind of another creature, let alone three others at the same time. And then there were the amaroq. And from when all this insanity had begun, with the wivre.

"I think I get it," I finally spoke. "When that thing appeared above me in the park, I could feel inside of its heads. Like a faint glimpse. I remember feeling how it, they, felt. But not much else."

"That creature was Ascalon," he replied. "As your skills develop," he continued, "I believe it will be easier for you to reach into them, and you will be able to dig deeper into all levels of their mind. With some of the more simple-minded summons, you will be able to control their every action completely."

He paused again. "That begins the problem, however, of how to start teaching you. Summoners and Guardians spend decades learning about the different animals here on Earth and from the Chaos Realm. There is an ancient text we use, thousands of years old, called the Bai Ze Tu. Although much of it is still incomplete, the pages stolen throughout various times in history, the pages we do have describe all the creatures of the Chaos Realm, their attributes, and how to control and conquer them. Guardians focus on their identification, their powers, and how to neutralize or defeat them. Summoners do the same, but they also study their character and personality so as to be better able to access inside of their mind."

"Okay, so, you're saying we need to go get this book and—"

Edrick held up a hand with an annoyed look on his face. "It is not as simple as that," he said. "What remains of the book is housed in Citadel. No one has access to it outside of its library."

I scoffed. "You mean I can't go online and look this thing up right now? Come on," I said, walking back to the house.

Edrick frowned. "What do you mean 'look it up online'?" I could hear him jog a few steps to catch up to me.

I crossed the small yard that led from the field back into the house. For a change, I felt confident, cocky even. I liked the feeling of knowing something more than this mystery man. Edrick seemed confused as he silently followed me. I left the staff leaning up against the counter as I went into my bedroom and grabbed my laptop. Bringing it back out into the kitchen, I set it down on the table while I took a seat. As soon as the desktop opened up, I paused. "What was the name of the book again?"

"The Bai Ze Tu. However, I do not believe—"

"Got it!" I declared triumphantly. I had typed the best spelling I could think of as he said it. My spelling wasn't too far off, at least not bad enough that the search engine couldn't figure out what I wanted. The first thing that showed up, of course, was a Wikipedia entry. I clicked on it and began to read it to Edrick. "The *Baí Zé* was encountered by the Yellow Emperor or *Huáng Dì* while he was on patrol in the east. Thereafter the creature dictated to *Huáng Dì* a guide to the forms and habits of all 11,520 types of supernatural creatures in the world, and how to overcome their hauntings and attacks. The emperor had this information written down in a book called the *Bái Zé Tú*. This book no longer exists, but many fragments of it survive in other texts." I coughed. "Over eleven-thousand different creatures?"

I thought Edrick would be pleased that I could find this information. Instead, as I turned to look at him, his face fell gray and dark. Tension lines appeared as his eyes stared hot and angrily at the computer screen. Without taking his eyes off of it, he grabbed the other seat and sat down beside me. That's when I noticed he was trembling slightly. "That is not possible," he barely spoke. "Those texts are sacred. They were supposed to remain a secret. If you could find them so easily…" He ran his hand through his hair. His expression bounced from shock to anger. Blue fire burned in his eyes as his face glowed bright with rage. "This means someone, or someone's, have broken their vows. They have exposed our secrets. They… are traitors."

The tension and aggression radiating from him was palatable. Hesitantly, I looked over, forcing myself not to scoot away. Edrick sat back in the chair and crossed his arms, his eyes glued to the screen, though I don't think he was actually looking at it. His eyes appeared locked, as if he were looking through it.

"I'm sorry," was all I could think of to say.

Edrick shook his head slowly. "It makes me wonder how many more of our secrets have been revealed to the common world," he mused softly, and I could barely hear him.

"Like what?" I asked, curious now as to what events he was referring to.

Edrick stared past the screen a moment more before his eyes snapped back into the present. "I suppose this part of my job will be easier then," he said, gesturing to the computer. "Let us see how much information this machine can reveal."

We spent a good while trying to look up the actual book, but besides a few pages in either Chinese or Japanese, none of which I could read, it didn't really seem to exist. "Can I ask," I started, trying to break the silence. "Are all of these mythological creatures I grew up learning about actually real?"

Edrick frowned. "Which do you mean?"

"Well, you said dragons are real," I began. "Does this also mean that creatures like unicorns and fairies are as well?"

Edrick nodded slowly. "Yes, but do not think that the simple and gentile attributes you know of refer to the same creatures. Most of those beings from the Chaos Realm are deadly. They have to be. We do not know much about their home. We have surmised over the years that the Chaos Realm is aptly named because it is a place too difficult for anything that we know of from Earth to survive there. That is why the Lyndwyrm tried to take control of our world."

My brain stopped listening when he admitted that unicorns and fairies were real. It was still hard to believe even though I knew at this point

Edrick would not lie about anything that he told me. "Do you think I could still learn about them if I looked them up?"

Edrick still seemed distracted and irritated, and it came out in his voice, which instantly made me feel like an irritating child for even asking the question. "I suppose you could try," he said, "though I would take anything you find with a grain of salt. Besides whether or not they are a creature of the Chaos Realm, I do not know if their information would be accurate."

"Well, maybe you could tell me the name of something you are familiar with. I can look it up and if it looks like that thing, we can practice me trying to summon that?"

Edrick thought about it for a moment. Then a small, wry smile appeared. "Alright, try to find a cynnamolgus." He spelled it out for me, and I quickly did a search.

I opened up several pictures. Edrick looked carefully at each in turn before pointing to one. "This. It is not a perfect representation, but it is close."

The odd-looking bird had a more common name I could actually pronounce — cinnamon bird. It looked like a rather large bird, golden brown in color, its feathers striated with darker chocolates and a few light gold highlights. In the image, its wings spread open, wide and broad. Its long neck reached up with a head ending in a short but broad and strong beak. Between its eyes rose feathered decorations, like a crest and horns. Two other decorative feathers flowed upwards and back. Its tail appeared medium length, a few longer feathers flowing out from the end of it like that of a rooster.

"Alright," I said after studying the image the best I could. "I think I can remember what this looks like."

We stepped back outside and made our way out to the field, away from the house, and hidden behind a line of trees from the road. No one could see what we were doing.

In the middle of an old corn field left to weed, surrounded on three sides by rows and rows of bare apple trees, Edrick had me stop. "Now, I do not know for sure if this is the best way to teach you," he began, "but you do not have the luxury of time and skilled teachers as I had. Try, then, to visualize and feel what the cinnamon bird is like, how it feels, thinks, smells."

I stood with my eyes closed for a few minutes. I wasn't sure what I was doing. Before, Ascalon had just appeared. I don't remember doing anything. And I was feeling way too many things to remember on any specific thought or emotion. Focusing as hard as I could, I pictured the bird sitting in a tree, flying. I imagined it sipping a cup of cider with cinnamon sticks sticking out of it. The last image made me giggle.

I cracked open my eyes and saw Edrick standing right in front of me, scowling. "What are you doing?"

"Sorry," I said through another giggle. "I had a funny image just go through my head."

His expression didn't change. "Are you trying? You can ill afford to make a game of this."

My grip on the staff tightened. "Yes," I said, a little annoyed. "I just don't know what I am supposed to be doing, or if I am doing it right. And you're not offering much help," I muttered the last under my breath.

"Do you remember what you were thinking the last time?"

Did I? I had never seen that creature before. All I remembered was the panic, the fear. I had thought….

"I thought I was going to die."

"And?"

"And… I remember being very aware of the staff in my hands, and feeling like it wouldn't be enough, but I knew I had to hold onto it and not let go—"

I never finished my sentence. Edrick moved like lightning before me. I could hear the woosh and hiss of his sword clearing its scabbard, though I didn't actually see it. A fire flared in his eyes as his face grew dark. I didn't even have time to scream as he brought the sword over his head in two hands. In one fluid motion, he swung it down and to the side as if to cut off my head.

My grip on the staff grew so tight, I felt like my fingers had melded inside of the wood.

All this happened in a second, yet again, it felt like it was slower. And I could feel it, the swooning, lightheadedness from before. I shut my eyes tightly, feeling as if I were about to fall over. Yet…

Something knocked my body backwards. I fell hard on my back into the muddy soil, the staff landing hard against my chest. A large shadow stood before me, blocking the sun and casting everything around me in darkness.

I could hear Edrick shout something, though I couldn't make out what he said. The creature interrupted him with a horrible trumpeting sound that reverberated through my head. With a groan, I sat up, watching as the thing took a step away from me. A massive tail swung up and over its head in a woosh, and I could almost hear more than see as the force of it dragged the creature forward a few feet.

From the other side, I could hear a man grunt, before the beast screamed again.

Pain arched through my already throbbing head and neck.

"Brianna!"

"Edrick!" I shouted back, struggling to my feet. My head felt funny again. I leaned heavily against the staff. I was angry. No, enraged. I wanted to stab it. No, stab…him.

I shook my head and looked at the creature. It turned slightly, looking back over at me.

Large, black eyes took me in, and I could not only see myself, but in a way like looking through someone else's eyes. An almost human face sprang from the strange, flat black and gray carapace. Human, but for the stubby nose, strange eyes, and massive mouth filled with rows of teeth. I could feel it. Confused. Hungry.

"Brianna, watch out!"

Somehow, I knew what was going to happen even before Edrick said anything. I jumped to the side, nearly tripping on a rock as a thick, crimson streaked scorpion tail smashed down into the spot I had just stood.

I felt terrified, but even more so, angry. "No!" I shouted up at it, less out of fear, and more the tone someone would use scolding a dog.

The creature let out a strange, guttural hiss, cocking its head as it brought its tail back up, twitching it from side to side.

I looked deep into its eyes. I felt it, as I had before the others. It's mind! It's rage at being ripped from familiar surroundings. The insatiable hunger it felt. And deep, deep down, almost a primordial fear…

"No!" I screamed again, this time in pain. The beast before me trumpeted painfully. It whipped around, stabbing wildly at the ground in all directions. I collapsed to my hands and knees, puking. More stabs of pain arched through my body, but I knew it wasn't my body. Through gasps and heaves, I begged it to stop. I begged Edrick.

Neither could hear me until sometime later, I felt a warm, numbing blanket over my mind.

I don't know what happened but the next thing I knew, Edrick was holding my shoulders tightly. I had been crying. My face was wet, everything I saw blurry. He must have sensed something because he lifted my face a little, just enough so that he could look into my eyes where I sat.

"Brianna, are you hurt?"

I sniffled and shook my head. "No, not me. But... I could feel that thing, hurt, dying." Something brought the feeling back up into the front of my mind. I suddenly felt fresh, hot tears welling. "I'm sorry, Edrick, I tried."

"I know," he said. His hand petted my hair. It was soothing but in seconds, he seemed to startle himself and put his hand back on my shoulder. "I apologize for feigning an attack. It seems your abilities right now are primal; they activate in order to protect you. I promise you, Brianna, that I would never truly hurt you. It was an act to draw out your power."

I didn't say anything. I didn't know how to feel. I still felt raw and sensitive inside. I still felt confused. I figured this would be some simple but weird training exercise. Why hadn't I summoned the cynnamolgus? Why had that...

I had thought "thing," but it felt too cold, harsh. It hadn't been just a thing. Sure, it had tried to attack me, but it was scared. It was... had been... a living being. It had feelings. It felt pain and fear. It was terrified of dying.

"You do not know what that was." He paused, as if searching for words. "It was a robust being called a manticore. It would have been difficult to fend off, but I had an opening when you distracted it. Remember that if you ever need to summon one again. Manticore."

I ran a sleeve of my coat across my nose. "It was in so much pain, Edrick. It was scared, hungry. It didn't understand why it was here."

Edrick's face fell further. "I... did not know you could feel all that. I suppose I thought... that you could simply tell it what to do. Nothing more."

I looked around him, but the manticore was gone.

"They begin to dissipate after they are… gone," Edrick said, knowing what I was thinking. "Their energy is a disruption to this existence. When they… pass, they dissolve and their energies, we assume, end back up in the Chaos Realm."

I was a bit glad that I didn't have to see it dead. I probably would have broken down crying again. This way, my mind felt as if everything had been only a bad dream. Even though deep down, I knew it wasn't. "I… I don't think I can do this."

Edrick cocked his head a bit, his eyes narrowing in question.

"I don't think I can be a Summoner, Edrick. That was too… painful. I feel like if that happens all the time, I'm going to end up going insane. I can't stand feeling the pain. The… dying."

His grip on my shoulders tightened. "You can do it," he said, his voice strong but soft. "I am not sure how to teach you. I suppose you will have to figure that out on your own. But I remember reading about mental defenses Summoners can use to help block—"

I waved my hand for him to stop, shivering. And it wasn't from the weather. "Let's go back to the house for now, okay? I just need a break."

It was more than just a break. I went inside and immediately found an old bottle of bourbon. It was left over from the last time Mark had come over when I actually liked him. Edrick watched, arms crossed, face dark and disapproving as I poured myself a generous shot. Okay, it was more like three shots in the glass — and I painfully downed it all in a single go. I coughed a little. I wasn't much of a drinker, and I would typically have a sweet drink or two, maybe some wine. Nothing hard like bourbon. That was Mark's drink. But it was all I had.

I sat down at the table. I knew I didn't want to think about it, but at the same time, I felt like I had to learn more about the manticore. I had been inside its mind, after all. And though the memory of it still scared me, I knew there was more to it than just the fear it elicited.

Edrick stood behind me and off to the side, arms stilled crossed and leaning against the counter. He didn't say anything as I looked the creature up online on a few different sources, reading about it. Most of the pictures had it all wrong. Did ancient people really see manticores this way? Or had someone saw the creature, and then told another person who drew the manticore based on what the first person had said.

Curious, I looked up the next one I remember Edrick saying. Dragon. I knew what a dragon was, yet the variety of them that came up were ridiculous.

I tried to think of the name of another creature he had told me about. The alcohol was kicking in and I started feeling relaxed and warm. I seemed to have forgotten about the painful experience and was caught up in looking at different creatures.

"Wivre," Edrick suggested, finally breaking the silence. "Look up wivre."

It took a few tries since that seemed to be an older name for the creature. The more common name seemed to be wyvren. Again, dozens of images popped up, but none of them seemed to have it completely right. I skimmed through the descriptions and shook my head. "These are all wrong, aren't they?"

"Yes," Edrick replied. "If I have the chance, I will find a way to bring you some of the Bai Ze Tu to study."

"I don't want to be a Summoner," I said, this time with a bit more conviction. The bourbon burned my gut, but it brought a strange clarity to my mind. "I'm sorry. I thought I could do this. But my world is already upside down. I can't do this and hold down a steady job. What will I do about housing, food, when I get sick…?" Edrick sat down beside me and it finally hit me. "Wait, where do you live? How do you afford things?"

"I do not live anywhere," he answered. "I get food as I need it. Sometimes I find it, sometimes people give me food. There have been a few times I needed to… convince others for food, medicine, or supplies."

"Convince? What, do you trick them? Threaten them?"

"I never threaten another human being unless it is necessary," he said. "Part of our skill set is the ability to speak to others in a way that convinces them that helping you is something they want to do, even if that is not their initial intent."

"You trick them," I grumbled.

I caught the beginning of a wince as he turned his head. "I do what I must to protect mankind. If I must... trick... someone for food, it is a small price to pay."

"So that is how you are tricking me to become a Summoner?" In the back of my mind, I hadn't wanted to say that. But the bourbon—

"I have not tricked you at all."

"Saying my life is dependent on being some weird magic person, I'd say that's tricking me." My mouth started going off. I could feel my face begin to glow. I couldn't stop myself as my mouth continued without reason. "How do I know you aren't manipulating these creatures? You seem to always be around when they pop up. I bet," I began, pointing a finger at him, "if you really stepped out of my life, like, really fucking left me alone, I'd be fine. Everything would go back to normal."

Edrick cringed at the profanity before his eyes narrowed. His face turned solid, hiding how he truly felt, what he genuinely wanted to say. "I swore to you I would protect you."

I stood up fast, fighting the wooziness in my head. "But what if to protect me you needed to trick me? I mean, I only have known you for a week." I shook my head slowly. "What if all of this is really made up from my concussion. Or..." *Or what if the accident had been worse, and I was in a coma?*

"Brianna, where are you going?"

"Please leave me alone," I pleaded, walking towards the bedroom door. "I... I need to think..."

He stood up quickly, grabbing me firm by the elbow. "Brianna, I need you to understand—"

"No!" I snapped. "If you're really not manipulating me, then go away. I need to be alone for a while."

Edrick nodded his head once. "Fine, I will —"

"—not stand outside of the house," I blurted out. "You want to prove to me that all of this is real, that you aren't just tricking me, then go away. For a while."

"How much time —"

"—a long while." Turning, I walked into the bedroom, slamming the door behind me. I leaned against it, my heart racing, my head hot and spinning from the booze. For several minutes I stood there, my ears straining for any sound, my chest tightening. Too much. This was all too much for me to handle.

Tears had started forming in the corners of my eyes when I finally heard the scratch of a chair being pushed back in, followed by steps. The front door shut quietly. I closed my eyes, waited for as long as I could. Part of me wanted to run after him, apologize. I was scared, terrified. He *had* been the only thing so far that had kept me safe. But the world... the world had grown crazy since he had arrived in my life. After what seemed like hours, I brushed the tears away, opened the door, and peeked.

The kitchen was empty. The chair had been pushed in. The door was shut tight.

I couldn't see anyone standing from any of the views I had out the window. An uneasy feeling began to settle on me. Walking over to the windows, I looked out further.

Nothing.

Were it not for the staff still leaning up against the counter, I would have believed that I had exorcised the whole nightmare from my consciousness.

I knew however, no matter how much I tried to deny it, it was all real.

I'm not sure why I walked extra quietly back to the bedroom. Everything seemed unnaturally still. Part of the reason had to be due to everything that had happened lately. I felt hyper aware. On edge.

A nap. I needed a nap. Desperately. I felt mentally and emotionally fried. The other times I had felt the minds of the Chaos Realm creatures, I had passed out. With manticore, I felt as if I were about to pass out, but I didn't. Was it because it was a weaker creature? Was I getting stronger? A little of A and B?

I didn't even care that dirt, a bit of mud, and now grass stains still clung to my clothes. I flopped onto my bed.

My eyes fell shut quickly. But my ears stretched their sense. My mind whirled.

Alone, quiet, I recalled the manticore's feelings. Fear and shock dominated its mind. And when the small creature began to attack it, it hurt, grew angry. It had only been trying to find food when it had been ripped from its home to the strange place that hurt it.

Killed it.

I had to sleep. Shaking my head, I flipped over in bed, face down. I had to think of other things. The pillow felt so soft and plush on my face. The bed absorbed my body, and I could feel myself slowly melting, relaxing. I ached from the spill I took. I hurt, but not at all like from the car accident.

Not at all like the pain of dying. The fear. The loneliness. Not understanding why.

Was that how Kara felt as she died?

Grunting, I turned over to my side.

Have to think of something else.

I tossed and turned for… I don't know how long. I fought my brain for what seemed like hours. I cried. I screamed. Everything seemed to be changing, too fast, and not for the best. I wanted to go back to a week ago, to the life I once had. Somehow, I knew that would never happen. So, what was left for me in the future? My mine reeled with events, while at the same time I tried to think of other things. Happier things. *Would I ever be able to do those things again?*

CHAPTER 6

The dream faded. As fast as I woke, the vision dissipated, with not a fragment to remember. I tried to recall if it was even a good one or a nightmare. *Maybe better I forgot it,* I thought, opening my eyes. I reached for my cell phone that always sat on my nightstand. For a moment I panicked when I couldn't feel it. And then I remembered.

I'd lost that. Along with my purse, money, cards, ID. And lost Kara. My job. My car.

My fucking sanity!

I screamed into a pillow.

When I ran out if breath, I sat up in bed. I felt like crap. The bourbon had left an odd taste in my mouth, and a tension in my head. Well, it was either that or whatever my dreams had been about.

For several minutes I just sat. I didn't feel like changing out of my dirty clothes. The bed kept getting dirty, I almost didn't care anymore. I could have hopped in the shower.

None of that would change anything.

Numb, I walked into the kitchen, taking my coat with me. A walk. Maybe a walk would—

I stopped in front of the staff. My first thought was *burn it.* A slight shudder ran through my body, as my mind reeled again at what I had felt in the mind of another. Shaking my head with a sigh, I headed towards the door. One hand was on the knob, the door opened about a foot.

The feeling of being alone. Helpless. In the dark of night. It would be light out for another hour. But the way my life was going… the amaroq…

Swearing like a sailor under my breath, I walked back over to the staff and snatched it. I didn't want it. I wish I never knew of it. But I had also chased away the one person who knew what the hell was going on. The only person who I was beginning to believe could help me.

The staff, for being so long and oddly shaped, felt comfortable in my hand as I began a brisk pace through the yard towards the now empty field. Behind me, the sun sank lower in the west giving me maybe an hour of light before dark.

I just needed to take a quick walk. I needed space. I needed freedom.

I stared at the ground as I walked, hardly noticing the cold air that formed a fog around my head with every breath. Without realizing it, I came up on an area where flattened grass and broken weeds laid. Scattered about, clumps of sod lay bare, now dry in the waning sun.

A deep chill ran through me. I thought it was the cold. Bending over to lay the staff down so I could close my coat...

I stood up fast. It wasn't the cold. I could still feel it, like it was a part of me. Would it be that way forever?

"I'm sorry." Swallowing back the tears, I stared at the grooves and sod. I mourned for the manticore.

But hadn't it tried to kill me?

Was it?

I remember sitting around a bonfire over the summer at Kara's house. Night was closing in as we talked about girl things while sipping beers. I felt something odd on my calf and reflexively, I slapped it. I remember the burning, stinging pain as I yelped, then howled in pain. The bee sting lasted for several days. I don't know what happened to the bee, but I imagine it didn't survive.

Back then, it was just something that happened. I don't know why it came to me now, other than, I think I understood. It was only defending itself. The manticore hadn't intentionally been trying to kill. Somehow, I knew if it wanted to, it would have done so. It had only been trying to defend itself.

Hurriedly, I zipped up my coat, then picked up the staff from the ground. Not much farther away there was a small vernal swamp that formed a small, still pond, and a crick no more than a foot across and a few inches deep. I had found it the year before during a hike. No one, I wagered, knew it existed, so I would be alone, remote.

I tried to focus on each step over uneven ground as every moment it grew darker and darker. Fatigue and tears fought back. The staff felt heavier, colder in my bare hand.

Twenty minutes from my apartment, and through a tall patch of wild, thorny wild roses, I found my vernal swamp. The surface was covered in the faintest layer of clear ice that looked like glass under the rising moonlight. Frost sparkled on the dead weeds and brush around it. Off to the left, there was a large boulder I liked to sit on, with two smaller one's side-by-side in front of it, acting as a foot stool. I made my way to the icy cold boulder. A small patch facing the south still held a touch of the sun's warmth, and I perched myself there, resting the staff against it.

The sun finished its descent, the moonlight giving the world new shadows. The surface of the pond shone back its silvery brilliance. Beneath the surface, it was like a dark hole that fell away to who-knew-where. If it were similar to the other vernal ponds in the area, it couldn't have been more than a few feet, waist-high at the most. But right now, I imagined it to be the deepest hole in the world.

I turned my head, my eyes falling on the staff. Bobbles gleamed, the shard of metal appearing sharper than it did in the daylight. "I don't know what to do," I whispered into the night. "I just want my life back. But how could that ever happen? Everything is already so different."

"Man has choice," a smooth voice, both soft and reverberating spoke, "yet one's past cannot be rewritten."

I nearly fell off the boulder, my eyes frantically searching the world before me. "Who's there? I—"

"I know you, Summoner," the voice interrupted.

A shift out of the corner of my eye brought me to the thing sitting atop the ice. The ice never broke, but it should have. No way could the smooth, thick, serpentine beast sit on it without breaking. "Who—"

"The Summoner's past is set as firm as the stone it sits upon," the beast continued, lowering its head out of the trees. All I could make out of the snake-like head were round eyes that revealed twin moons. "The dragon knows its breath, its step. He will hold the last of the Summoners, but fall from them, it will."

I couldn't help myself from trembling. "Dragon... you're saying, he will find me? Where can I go, hide?"

"Terrible falls kill the weak, Summoner. The strong survive, though never unscathed, born anew as the past dies."

The being radiated a power, a feeling older than anything around me, even that of the boulder. I realized with a start that I couldn't feel inside of it. Well, just barely. It was old. Calm. It was— "Who are you?"

"The weak dies, the choice lies in strength," it hissed. "The weak die, the strong reborn, that is unwritten."

Something shifted in my thoughts. A sense of... finality.

Like with Edrick, everything happened so fast, I couldn't think, only react. The coiled creature lunged at me. I fell to the side, intentionally, landing in frozen mud. My hand tipped the staff, sending it tumbling with me.

A fiery rage filled my mind. The need to kill.

Death.

The weak dies!

My thoughts were still on the manticore as a hissing filled my ears. The world around me seemed to pop, but in a way, you couldn't hear it but feel it, kind of like when your ears popped during pressure changes. But this popping was greater than any I could remember.

I scrambled for the nearest tree on all fours, struggling to breathe. Out of one eye, I saw something large appear, crushing through the thin ice, stopping with a plopping, sucking sound of mud. Two beings cried, one like a brain shattering trumpeting, and one with a hiss that felt paralyzing. With a grunt, I scrambled to my feet, one hand against the rough, papery bark of a birch, the other on the smooth, warm staff.

My eyes brought hope to my brain that the manticore had been resurrected, that it hadn't really died. Whatever part of my brain could sense the beings before me knew better. This manticore stood slightly larger, its movements quicker, more intentional. Its mind rang with a terrifying rage. It knew what arched before it. It reared on back legs, blocking its human-esque face with giant, talon-tipped paws. The red banded scorpion tail shot forward.

The serpentine beast screamed in frustration. "The weak will die! The weak will die!"

Distracted by the weaving, darting head, the manticore and myself didn't notice as coils from the rear of the creature wrapped themselves around the manticore. One swept it off of its feet, and I could hear and feel, more than see, as it crashed into the freezing mud.

"The weak will die! The weak will die!"

"No, stop!" I shrieked as the manticore tried to trumpet again. I could feel the tightness of an anxiety attack crushing my lungs, my back, my—

No, it wasn't me, as I sank to my knees. Coils snaked up the manticore's fallen body. As it exhaled, it couldn't draw in anymore air. More of the snake thing's body continued to wrap itself around the manticore, pinning legs and claws that were unable to tear and shred.

It was happening again. Though different, slower. I could feel the racing heart, the aching, burning lungs struggling for air. The sharp tightness crushing limbs, breaking ribs—

One part continued to flail. I stared up at the strange, dimming moon, and stabbed. I could feel the stinger make contact. The beast continued to scream words I didn't understand. It didn't matter. I stabbed at it, over and over. I could feel the pain slacking, but it wouldn't be enough. The damage was done. It just wasn't enough...

I gasped as something pulled me from the darkness. I screamed, overwhelmed. Crying.

"The harm you do will end with your death," came a weak hiss. Through tear blurred eyes, I could see the head only a few feet from me, the eyes dimmer, but still showing me the moons. "But at the birth, you will be the redeemer. The weak will die. The weak will die—"

Not knowing what else to do, I screamed at it. Screamed so hard, I could feel my throat growing raw.

Everything fell to silence as the long, silver blade pierced its head.

It was too quiet. So, I cried.

I didn't know if I felt furious or yet again grateful. I know I was in pain, inside and out, shivering, as I hiked back to the house as quickly as I could. It helped that I wasn't burdened by the weight of the staff. Without a word, Edrick picked it up. He followed my pace, never more or less than a few feet from me. As I panted, my teeth chattering and trying to push down my sobs, I could hear the rustling and creaking of his armor, his large satchel, and tinkling of the staff's bobbles.

I could feel them before I even reached the house. Many minds, patient yet trembling with anticipation. I knew they were waiting for me. I could also feel the hesitation rise as they sensed Edrick.

"Fuck off!" I screamed hoarsely into the night. I wasn't in the mood. I felt terrified. Wild. I would summon a hundred manticore if even one of the amaroq showed itself. Hell, I almost wished one would. I'm sure that would fuck up my mind more than anything else. Maybe then I could be free of this hell that was apparently now my life.

I stormed into the house, swiping my hand across the light switch. Nothing.

"Go fucking figure! You assholes!" I shouted, though I could feel myself losing my voice.

Like I had lost my mind.

I didn't want to acknowledge his presence, yet I could tell Edrick came in behind me, cringing. Behind me on the table, I could hear him rummaging through his bag and, less than a moment later, a dim, buttery glow filled the kitchen. Which was just as well as it made it easier for me to find a clean glass and the last of the bourbon bottle I had put away. Still in my coat, clothes caked with warming mud, I plopped into a chair and filled the glass. No shots tonight. I wanted to destroy my mind. I wanted to erase everything. Trembling, I raised the glass to my lips and drank. The booze burned my already raw throat. It hit my stomach like a stream of fire. Not even a third of the way through the glass I put it down, already feeling my stomach recoil.

Edrick took a seat across from me. He watched me, his face stone, his eyes neutral. The lamplight danced across his face, revealing nothing. As if trying to prove something I didn't even know, I tipped the glass back again until less than half remained. I gasped, wiping at my mouth and chin with a muddy sleeve. In a raspy voice, I said, "You fucking lied. Just like you have to everyone else."

He cocked his head slightly, eyes narrowing.

"You fucking followed me!"

"I did not," came his soft, careful reply. "I had made camp nearby when I heard the trumpeting of the manticore. I... feared you were in trouble. So, I came running." He nodded. "I know you do not wish to hear it, but you handled yourself well against the phython."

"It died," I hissed, squeezing the glass tightly with both hands. "Don't you fucking get it? Another one died. They all die. Everything! And guess who gets to fucking feel that? Over, and over and over—"

"You had no choice," he broke in. "I know it hurts. Yet with time, practice, you will learn how to keep your summons alive, if that is your wish. However—"

"You have no idea," my voice quivered. "How many monsters, how many people have you killed? You've never felt a single death. Don't know how it feels to die inside with them, then to feel the pain of coming back into your mind. Alive. So, don't," I stabbed at his direction with a finger, "fucking tell me you know how it feels."

A slight blush rose to his cheeks and for the first time, Edrick cast his eyes to the side. "You are right. I do not understand. And I never could."

"Right," I muttered. I picked up the glass to finish it, but I could already feel the other two-thirds working. My stomach begging me, *not yet.*

We sat in silence for a good long while. My fingers played with the grooves and cuts in the glass. The smoothness of the surface. *Smooth, like the ice of the lake. The sides of the other creature. The…*

I let out an exasperated sigh. The blanket of drunkenness had begun to lay across my mind. Deadening emotions. Blunting the edges of my problems. It was easy to see now why so many people took to drinking after difficult moments in their life. I wondered if I was fated to be one of them. Fated. My own curiosity was killing me. "Fine. What the hell is a phython?"

Edrick took his time meeting my eyes. There was a sadness I'd never seen before in them. Sadness? Or concern? How much better would be if I could get inside the minds of other humans, instead of monsters. Then again, was he even human?

"They were commonly summoned long ago during the time of ancient Greece," he began. "Summoners would call them forth for the virgin oracles to speak with on behalf of the Greeks. Many remained quite content with offerings of food and shelter, becoming one of several cases over the millennia of humans actually co-existing with creatures from the Chaos Realm. They could somehow prophesize the fates of men, with an alarming degree of accuracy.

"Existence of any monsters however is unacceptable by oath. Ancient Guardians would slay phythons as much as they could, many times having to slaughter the temple priests, oracles, and guards in the process. Eventually, other religions sprung forth, with the help of denouncing the oracles themselves. It has been a long time since any phython has come to Earth."

I knew I should have been shocked, but on this side of drunkenness, I didn't care.

Edrick looked down at his hands folded on the table. "Brianna, I know it hurts, yet this is extremely concerning. I have never heard of a case where phython presented itself without a summoning. Actually, I have not heard of the presence of a phython since the year 200 BC and have never seen one myself outside of textual drawings. Its presence here, in New York is… unsettling." He paused before looking at me. Those blue-gray eyes trapped me, and for a moment, I could feel myself sobering. "When I reached you, both the phython and manticore were locked in death, yet the phython continued to speak until I killed it. Do you remember any of that?"

Not liking the feeling of sobering up one bit, I finished the drink in my hands before nodding. "Yeah."

"This is important, Brianna. Did it speak to you at all before that moment?"

"Yeah. But it was like, all weird and stuff." I tried to remember, but at the moment, I was feeling both fuzzy and a bit nauseous. Maybe a whole glass of bourbon wasn't such a hot idea. "Stuff about dying and being born and stuff. Look," I pushed my empty glass away. "I kinda just wanna go to bed, ya know?"

"Brianna." With a speed I didn't see, he reached across the table and grabbed my hand. "This really cannot wait. I need you to remember as much as you can." He glanced at the cup now by his wrist and scowled. "Please."

"I… I really don' remember," I muttered. Part of me wanted to pull my hand away. The other part felt good having something strong holding onto me, even if it was just my hand. "I think it knew I was a Summoner. And, yeah, it said something about like dragon."

"What about him?"

I closed my eyes to stamp down the sudden wave of nausea, but phython met me, those eyes with the silver moon staring right at me. "The Summoner's past is stone. That Dragon knows its breath and step.

55

Something like that." I kept my eyes closed, trying to listen to the words. They were garbled, soft, like a television with low volume and getting bad reception. "Somethin' about a fall killin' the weak. Abou' the strong being born but not not hurt or somethin'." I opened my eyes, realizing too late my mistake. "I'm gunna be sick."

I felt my hand being jerked and squeezed hard. I gasped, looking up at Edrick. His eyes locked mine with an intensity I'd never witnessed. The feeling of sobering up washed over me. Enough to push down the nausea. "What else did he say? We need to know!"

"I-I-I don't remember, honestly," I sputtered. "I was scared. Awed. I wasn't thinking. Its words confused me. They didn't make total sense." I wriggled my hand from his grasp. "I-I-I can't do this right now. I'm sorry. I… need to be alone."

Edrick grunted, cupping his chin in his hand, rubbing his jaw with a finger. "I know it is not your desire, Brianna, but I cannot leave you alone. I am sorry for any misfortune you believe that causes. Get some sleep. We need to talk in the morning."

Feeling like I had been dismissed, I lumbered my way to the bathroom to puke.

I didn't feel well. Nothing did.

CHAPTER 7

I felt like shit the next morning. The bourbon had been a terrible idea, doing nothing for me that I hoped it would. I barely slept as the pack of amaroq howled their unearthly cries all night long. Something about their presence kept anything electrical from working. I couldn't even listen to music or the television to block out the sounds. Their cries rang throughout my body, twisting my mind, bringing back all the fears I had ever had. The worst were of the manticores.

Edrick had asked sometime in the middle of the night if I could get inside their minds. I didn't even dignify the question with an answer. He seemed hesitant to chase them off and kill them, however.

I could feel them, like movement behind a curtain. I knew it was there, but I stayed away from it. I felt enough to know I didn't want to get closer. They wanted me. Dragon wanted me.

But why?

Several times during the night, the hooded figure watched me from outside my window. It was likely a manifestation of my fear and inebriated state. One time, it appeared at the foot of my bed like a horror troupe. I rolled out of bed and tried to grab it, corner it. But a soon as I got close enough, it faded away as if it never existed. And did it? I started seeing it when all of these troubles with monsters began. Perhaps it was a part of my subconscious expressing itself? But what did it mean, and what was I supposed to do with that piece of information?

Another possibility formed in my mind, becoming the most likely answer for the strange shade. The ghost of Kara, pissed I did nothing to help her, believing that I caused her death.

If all these monsters were real, did that mean ghosts were too?

It didn't make any sense. Nothing did. And that made it just that much harder for me to relax, let alone sleep.

Dawn came and at some point, the howling and cries had left. My brain felt so numb and exhausted, I didn't think I could sleep if I had tried. I tried to concede to the fact that this would be my new reality. I was going to have to get over the notion that I could ever live a normal life again, regardless of what I chose to do.

I wondered, not for the first time, if Edrick ever slept. He continued sitting at the table, sipping his strange coffee smelling concoction out of his fancy cup. With the amaroq gone, electricity returned, and so he had put away his oil lantern. Despite it being morning, the kitchen lights brightened the small room. Outside, the world remained as dark as my thoughts, though I doubt the cold rain would wash any of it away.

Before I could even sit down with my first cup of coffee for the day, Edrick spoke. "Do you remember anything more?"

I sighed, taking a sip as I slipped into a chair. I was still wearing my clothes from the day before. I just couldn't fathom a shower without nursing the hangover first with some coffee. "I don't even remember what I told you."

"I believe this to be a matter of life or death. Yours." His drink sat to the side, the cup still full. I wondered if he had drunk it at all. "Brianna, I do not wish for you to die. You are too important. You are special. But I cannot help you if—"

"All I remember," I began, my nose buried in the steam of my cup, "was how confusing the phythons words were. That first I would die. Then something about the strong being born, but not... unscathed. That the past was set, but I think the future unwritten." I took a sip, honestly trying my hardest to recall. *Dragon.* "Dragon knows who I am. Something about him holding the last Summoner, but then there will be a fall..."

"'The harm you do will end with your death,'" Edrick quoted what seemed word for word. "'But at the birth, you will be the redeemer. The weak will die.' I remember, word for word, what I heard."

I watched him, silent, waiting for the magic answer.

Taking ahold of his cup, he drained it in one swallow. "I cannot figure it out. I was hoping you would remember. At least, more of the beginning so I could figure out the entire prophecy."

"That's all," I replied hoarsely.

"One path could mean you will die, and then be reborn, in a literal sense. Though that is highly improbable"

He ran a hand through his hair. "I believe it could also mean your power could save you, that awakening it will allow you to live. Either way, we need to get you into hiding. Until, that is, we figure out why Dragon is willing to go to these lengths to capture you."

"Maybe he somehow knew I'm a Summoner," I said. Saying it out loud, admitting it, hurt. It meant that everything that had happened, everything that would, was because of this stupid curse. That I was what I recently discovered I didn't want to be. "Maybe he needs me to bring some more monsters into this world. Like we really need more."

"Or he wishes you dead, to prevent something," Edrick continued. "Perhaps he wishes to use you as bait for other Guardians. Either way, we need to leave." Standing up, cup in hand, he looked down at me, daring me to question his decision. I stared back at those now hard gray eyes and knew I would acquiesce. "Clean up and gather a small pack of whatever you need. I need to get you into hiding until we figure this out."

I sat sipping my cup. I didn't register the taste, the warmth on my sore throat. I barely realized, later, I was taking a hot shower, the water turning my skin a bright red.

Leaving.

What did that really mean?

It felt surreal, as if nothing else lately really had. Was this like a short leave until everything was sorted? Or was this a leave, kind of like a witness protection program kind of leave? Would I ever be back?

Would I care?

I had already dressed and begun the process of packing a large duffel bag before it hit me. Sitting on the bed heavily, I held my hand against my chest, gasping for breath.

What was I doing? Thinking? I couldn't just up and leave! Where would we go? What about my family? I realized with a start that I hadn't contact my family at all, especially my little sister, Elizabeth. And what of Mark? He would be back home any day now if he weren't already. As much as I wanted to be done with him, a small part felt I still needed to speak with him. I imagined him walking into the house with Edrick sitting at the table. I wondered what kind of confrontational disaster that would turn into.

The anxiety pain increased. I tried to clear my mind, breathe deeply, yet more questions flooded. What about my stuff? Rent? What would I do for money?

A heaviness creeped over my brain, hot, smothering. I fell back into the bed. I had never had an attack this bad. Panic began to weave its way in. One second, I worried I couldn't breathe, the next forcing myself to realize I was okay.

Shaking my head, I tried to clear the buzzing heaviness, the racing excitement as muscles coiled for attack—

A scream ripped itself from my throat literally a second before my bedroom window imploded. Glass and cold rain showered my body as I reflexively curled into a ball, covering my head with my arms. My bed creaked and bounced as something heavy landed on it. A breath, hot, moist, and acrid, loomed over me. I didn't want to look, I could feel, no, taste my fear.

"Get away from her!" Edrick roared. I didn't hear him race into the room, but I heard the scrape of the sword as he drew it.

The creature's thoughts changed, but it definitely felt no fear by his threat. "Ah, so the rumor is true. The little human girl has a Guardian. No matter. He said nothing of sparing you."

My eyes opened on their own. I stared up at the chest of some furred animal. The coat lay flat and sleek, a matte gray color with only the hint of a brindle pattern. Its head rose above me, though lowered. A vibration made the bed tremble, and I suddenly realized the feline-like beast was purring. On either side of my head, clawed paws, larger than my spread-out hand, speared my sheets, ruining them for good.

Terrified, I didn't dare move.

"Why does Dragon want her?" Edrick snarled. I could sense him moving closer.

I could also sense that the cat-thing knew this. The purr-vibration intensified, and its mind filled with mirth. "Dragon? I am not one of his weak little sycophants. No, the Shadow Man wants her. Alive."

Edrick's eyes narrowed in confusion. "The Shadow Man?"

"I'll not bother explaining," the cat-thing hissed, "as you'll be dead!"

I have no idea what made me do it. Maybe I'm stupid. I'm definitely not brave. A split second before it leapt, it thought about it. The complex senses could tell how much spring it needed, how wide to open its paws to grab Edrick. Keeping its claws fully extended. Even the fine muscles of its muzzle pulled back so as not to get in the way of teeth it knew it was going to sink into his flesh. As it launched itself from my bed, I reached out and grabbed the nearest front paw.

It would have been impossible for me to hold onto the monster. My hand and arm stung with the force with which it pulled so easily from my feeble grasp. But it was enough to off balance the perfect, intricate actions it had believed it would make.

Something between the scream of an alley cat, but deeper, and a lion's roar, escaped its muzzle. It knew, too late, its attack had been upset.

"Run!" I heard Edrick's voice cry out.

I heard a flurry of activity nearby as I rolled out of my bed. Scrambling to my feet, I raced out of the bedroom and adjoined living room. I could barely breathe as I tripped and stumbled over everything in my way. Out of the house. I had to get out of the house. As I reached the front door, my hand reached out and snagged the staff leaning against the table. Thankfully, I had put sneakers on after I had gotten dressed as I dashed out into the freezing rain. The butt end of the staff bounced across the mud and grass as I continued to slip and stumble.

Halfway across the yard I tripped over myself, falling sideways into the mushy lawn. Gasping, I lay there a moment as a horrific sound ripped across the property, the now all-too-familiar sense flooding my brain. Only a handful of seconds passed before something grabbed my arm, pulling me almost up to my feet.

"Brianna! Are you hurt?"

Using the staff to help me the rest of the way up to my feet, I shook my head, panting.

We both turned at the snarl behind us.

The cat creature stood taller than what it seemed in the bedroom. The size of a small horse, it slinked towards us like panthers I've seen on nature shows, except it favored its left side heavily. Even in the November rain, I could see blood oozing from a fatal slash stretching from its shoulder to halfway down its ribcage. A chunk of skin hung from its gray and brindled flank, exposing the muscle. It was dying, but not dead yet.

Edrick grabbed my arm and yanked me forcefully behind him. His hand left a bloody trail on my sweater. That's when I noticed the leathers near his right shoulder were shredded, crimson rivulets running down to his sword hand. "Get back!"

I stumbled behind him, clinging to his other arm for balance. "You're hurt!"

The cat beast panted as it slinked closer. Slitted, golden eyes burned into mine. "Don't think you're safe," it growled, taking another, lurching step. "You cannot hide from him. He will have—"

The ground to the side of the beast exploded. I yelped as something dark flew out of the ground. The cat screamed, tackled to the ground. In my mind, I could feel its life snuffed out as another mind invaded my consciousness.

"It is the wivre!" Edrick exclaimed, changing his grip, two hands on his sword. "That *is* one of Dragon's minions!"

The rain now fell in sheets as I stared at the monster from around his arm. The fingers of my left hand gripped the staff tighter. More than ever I felt as if it were nothing more than a small, stick of wood. I imagined it splintering. Ascalon. If only I could summon the same creature. For a brief second, I felt fear and pain, though not from me. Could I do it?

Under my hand, I could feel Edrick tremble slightly. I looked up as his face. Pinched in pain and fear, he panted slightly. If it hadn't been raining out, he'd be soaked in sweat. "Edrick," I spoke quietly, "you're hurt."

The wivre's massive head shot down and snagged the body of the cat beast in its maw. Tossing its head back, the feline disappeared from the world. With an earth-rumbling hiss, it turned to us, unfurling its wings. Wounds scored its pebbled skin, breaking up the muted yellow-striped, dull gray hide with patches of brownish-red scabs. If Ascalon had been the most powerful creature, how come the wivre wasn't dead? Had it killed Ascalon before I passed out?

I didn't think Edrick would be able to fight it off again. Not in his state.

I opened my mouth to bring this up to Edrick, but it was too late.

A roar erupted from Edrick as he raised his sword.

Days ago — had it only been days? — I didn't recall seeing all of the wivre. It rose now, towering over us from even this distance. It pulled the rest of its tail from the hole it emerged from. The tail tapered quickly to maybe the width of a pencil. Dark gray in color, it was the only part of the wivre covered in keeled scales. It looked rather useless until it snapped its tail to face us.

The crack made me scream, more than the force with which I was knocked backwards. Edrick fell on me with a grunt, the staff pinned between us. The wivre used the tail like a whip. And I didn't see it move at all!

My ears had popped, and all I could hear was a ringing as Edrick rolled off of me. Staggering to one knee, he raised his sword defensively in front of him. His body began quivering. Some of the leathers of his chest armor had been torn open, and already I could see blood weeping with the dripping rain.

Edrick looked back at me, his mouth moving but I couldn't hear what he was saying. His eyes grew large, the pupils nearly hiding the calm blue-gray I'd been growing used to. Those eyes glanced at the staff before turning back to the monstrosity. His lips continued to move as he renewed his grip on the sword. For the second time, I could see reddish runes glowing, yet they seemed to be brighter, pulsing.

Both man and beast were distracted as my adrenaline spiked. There was no running from the wivre. And I was tired of running. Tired of being hunted down. My breathing quickened as I got to my feet. I could vaguely hear the snake hiss as a downward stroke of its wings buffeted me. Edrick's lips continued to move, but the ringing in my ears grew worse.

I felt it before I saw it happen. In my mind, the long, whip-like tail wagged, relaxed, even though the muscles at the base were coiled with explosive power. I could feel the small human preparing his useless strike. This time would be different.

I didn't know what I did until it was too late. My feet stumbled in the mud, running. Shoulder to shoulder with Edrick, I looked to him. His wide eyes, tear-filled, panicked. One hand came off the sword, as if to reach for me. Almost out of sight, I saw the long, weeping wound from left hip to right shoulder.

I held the staff out in front of me as if attempting something. Swing it? Use it as a shield? I didn't think I planned at all for this. All I could think was, *Ascalon, summon Ascalon. C'mon, you winged bastard, and appear!*

I can't even count how many times I've cut myself in my life. Sharp knives. Paper cuts. Cat scratches. They always hurt, burned, stabbed. Something. If you had asked, I would have believed being cut open from leg to chest would have hurt like hell. Yet I felt nothing. A strange sensation, but I wouldn't call it pain. A sensation as if my arms and legs had turned into jelly. I didn't even stop as the tail drew back, winding up for another crack. Droplets of blood flung from its end, and I think some ended up on my face as it grew warm. Another's thoughts entered mine, and though I couldn't see it, I could hear the trumpeting of another damned manticore.

I don't recall falling to my knees as Edrick raced past me, screaming.

Warmth and something slick filled my hands. I guess I wasn't holding the staff anymore. Beyond the chaotic royal rumble of the wivre, manticore, and Edrick, I saw a shadowed figure racing towards me. Its consciousness also filled my numbing mind, but this seemed calm, soothing.

I didn't feel it, but I knew I now lay on my side, warm guts sliding from my dulled fingers. Shadows filled my vision as the darkest one leaned over me.

CHAPTER 8

Choking. Coughing. Buzzing and beeping.

Slow movements hindered by hands. Voices.

"Easy, easy," a woman cooed. "Almost done. Just try to relax."

I...

I was... wasn't I dead?

Something slid from my throat. Burning. Raw. Hacking. The torture finally ended, and I could see the hose as it came out of my mouth. It felt amazing to have it gone, though it left a raw, fatigued sensation in my throat.

Wasn't I dead?

Why was there a hose in my mouth?

Something pressed against my hand. Blurred, I watched various doctors and nurses muttering as they milled away in dull scrubs and coats.

"Here, sip this, honey. It's warm water. But go slow."

The hospital room grew in focus as I sipped slowly from the thin plastic cup. It took both of my hands to hold it, and the nurse helped guide my motions. It hurt somewhat going down, yet it felt better than the dry burning sensation it replaced.

"Better?" she asked, taking the cup gently from me. "I'm going to change some bandages and then you can rest."

I tried to nod, but didn't have the energy to do even that, only shiver. Warm blankets added their weight on me, soothing, comforting. My eyelids floated closed. I felt so tired, so weak, all I could manage to do was lay still and feel everything with a numb, warm glow as the nurse moved about, changing a myriad of bandages.

Why were there so many—

I gasped, too tired to open my eyes.

"Oh, I'm sorry sweetie, did I—"

I wasn't listening to the nurse. I could hear Edrick cry out, a tortured, piercing sound, like his soul was leaving his body. His voice faded, drowned by the trumpet of the manticore, the shrieks and hisses of the wivre. I could hear my ears ringing, my breaths coming in ragged, panting sounds. I listened as the shadow leaned over me. It touched me as it whispered words I'd never heard before. A chill coursed through my body, the cold burning where it touched my exposed entrails. Some of the shadow snaked out, touching my forehead.

Don't die. It's not time.

My body felt shattered.

I opened my eyes and gasped, startled. The room was different. Quieter. Softer. The lights had been dimmed to near darkness.

I thought I was dead.

I knew where I was, but I couldn't seem to think of the word, my mind still feeling numb. What had happened to me? Why couldn't I remember?

"Are you up for some visitations, sweetie? Your brother is here to visit you." The face of the nurse floated above me. Familiar, yet I also felt I'd never seen her before.

I swallowed, feeling my chapped lips crack. "Brother? I—"

"Hello, Brianna," I heard a familiar voice interrupt.

"If either of you needs anything, I'm just outside, or you can press the button," the nurse said, leaving my field of vision.

"Thank you so much," he replied pleasantly.

Footsteps came closer and I could hear the rusting of fabric as someone sat in a chair. I felt his warm breath on my skin, still cold feeling, as he leaned in. The smell of spices.

"Edrick?"

It looked like him, but not. His shoulder-length hair had been pulled back, held with a small strip of leather. That, and his eyes, were the only parts of him I recognized. I had only ever seen the man wearing leather armor, and that, in my mind, had become part of his identity. Now, I could see a familiar pair of jeans. He wore a thin coat over a bulky sweater that also looked oddly familiar. It was odd. He looked... normal. Handsome, even.

"That was the most stupid thing I have ever witnessed anyone doing," he growled slowly. "It is any wonder you are alive at all."

"What . . . happened . . ."

66

His severe expression seemed to crack, and a smile formed on his lips. "And it is good to see you alive, Summoner Brianna. I feared greatly for your survival. But promise me that you will leave the battles to me until such a time you are adequately trained."

I gently placed a weak hand on my pounding head. "I… I don't get it. I was dead, dying. And you… were hurt?" My eyes burned, so I closed them.

"Well, I cannot even begin to guess what you were thinking or trying to accomplish." I could hear him sit back in the chair and sigh. "As for the rest, my injuries were nothing more than I could manage with some bandages and stitches. Poultices of ancient herbs for a night, and I am almost back to full health."

"What…" I shuddered. I could see behind my closed eyes how dark the blood sat in my hands, the warm, slick weight—

A strong, gentle hand shook me from the memory as it rested on my own. "Your injuries were… catastrophic. I was saved by my leather armor, which, while I was injured by the wivre's tail, was blunted by design. You suffered several broken bones by the impact of the tail alone. Left hip, most of your ribs, and your collarbone cracked but remained otherwise intact. The more critical injury clearly was the… disembowelment."

I moaned, feeling now the burning, throbbing, tight pain across my entire front. "I… I thought I was holding my guts."

He nodded once in agreement. "You were."

Weakly, I rested my other hand on the sheet over my abdomen. Wincing at the slightest touch, I placed it back along my side. "So, then…"

Edrick frowned, his eyes narrowing slightly. "I am not sure what it was, but it kept you alive long enough to allow me to get you to help."

"But how—"

He shushed me, pulling his hand back. For a brief moment, I felt disappointed.

"I will tell you what happened, so no more questions. You need to rest.

"After you were struck down, I went after the wivre. The manticore you summoned seemed to have found it to be more of a threat than myself. We managed to greatly wound the wivre, but it again got away. I am positive it is working closely with Dragon. The manticore was gravely injured and passed on, so no, I did no harm to it." I could see his eyes searching my face. Was he worried about how I would feel about him killing another manticore? How would I feel about him if he had butchered another? Disturbing my train of thought, he continued. "When I turned to tend to you, that is when I saw the shadow. It spoke in a tongue I had never heard before. Immediately I realized it was attempting to help. I watched as it pushed your viscera back in, sealing them in enough. I saw your breath come back to your body. I am not sure what happened after. Either the wounds were too great for the beast, or it decided it had done enough before it vanished. I grabbed you and rushed you to the road. A stranger gave us a ride to the hospital, and I did not leave until I was denied further by the healers."

"You mean, the doctors?"

"Yes, doctors," he replied. "They said I was not of your family. That is when I assumed the role of your brother. I told them we were practicing for one of those gatherings people have, with the fake armor and weapons... people who would never be prepared to face a Chaos monster, though they pretend they are."

"Like, a cosplayer?"

"Yes. I told them we were attacked by what looked like a large dog or a wolf. You may want to stick to that lie," he smirked. "After, I made my way back to your home, where I hid both the sword and staff, and treated my wounds. I found a pile of men's clothing in your room; I am sorry for intruding in there."

"They're my... they're Mark's," I replied. Why had I hesitated to call him my boyfriend? "Have... have you seen Mark?"

Edrick cocked his head. "I am not sure if it is the same person. As I left with the weapons back to camp the next day, someone arrived. Upon seeing the destruction in the yard and front door, they rushed in, shouting your name. Perhaps that was your Mark."

Groaning, I closed my eyes. "He doesn't even know I'm here."

A warm hand gently squeezed mine. "Do not worry, Brianna. Your task now is to heal."

"But Mark—"

His voice seemed to change slightly as he gave my hand another quick squeeze. "Rest, Brianna. Think of nothing else now. Rest."

Angry voices woke me up.

Grimacing, I opened my eyes. The room remained dimmed. How long had I been asleep? Time in a hospital room felt... endless. Nonexistent. I felt worse, which probably meant they had reduced my pain meds.

But I felt more awake, alive. There had been dreams. Endless dreams. I couldn't recall them, which was a bit disturbing. Had they been important? Or were they just memories, taunting me, making me relive fears and pain?

I felt like crap. I ached and felt generally gross.

Awake. Hurting. But alive. And for some reason, a touch angry.

My eyes started to drift close when the voices broke through the haze. Loud, enraged voices muffled somewhat by the curtained glass door. The words at first remained unrecognizable but as the seconds passed, I could make out the speakers.

The kind nurse.

Edrick.

Mark.

My breath caught in my throat with the last, head swirling like a reverse toilet. All the memories and conversations flooded up to the forefront. All the time we spent together. His nagging insistence that we always do things together. His annoying, pointless conversations. His sharp, almost violent jealous streak. My god, why did I even start dating him to begin with? Swirling, too, flashed memories with Edrick. Monsters. Magic. Always there when dangers threatened me.

Part of me had hoped, as I gasped for breath, that my time with Edrick had been a long dream. Part of me realized I had almost forgotten about Mark. Part of me wondered if life with Mark would mean going back to normalcy.

Was it possible?

Was that what I really wanted?

Still dizzy with emotion, I looked through a small crack of the door not covered by the curtain into the hallway.

Mark stood the closest. I could only see half of his face, yet it glowed with rage. As his mouth moved in angry shapes, I realized that his voice boomed the loudest. White-knuckled fists pressed tightly against his thighs. If it weren't for the nurse standing before him, I wondered if there would be a fist fight. He looked as if he hadn't been home long, or, at the hospital too long. Thick, black hair appeared uncombed, wrinkles in his jeans, and I imagined his shirt under the sweater was as wrinkled as the pants. He took a step forward, his left hand shooting up, pointing a finger vehemently past the nurse.

The nurse, at least a foot shorter, stood her ground, and from here, it looked as if it would have taken a bulldozer to move her. Her face had started glowing red as well, her kind blue eyes narrowed threateningly as she spoke something quiet and aggressive in Mark's direction.

Behind her stood Edrick. Roughly the same size as Mark, he seemed at ease. Arms casually crossed, one hip leaning against the far wall of the hallway, a teasing smirk on his lips. He still wore Mark's pants and sweater.

My chest clenched. There stood Edrick, some kind of ancient warrior, who knew me, who had been with me when I had been hurt, wearing my boyfriend's clothes.

I sensed before I saw Mark turning his head, and I quickly looked away, my cheeks burning. What would I say? What *could* I say? Curious, I waited several seconds before glancing back out.

Mark began to gesticulate wildly with his hands as the nurse took a step closer.

Turning his head slightly, Edrick caught me staring at him. He gave me a lop-sided grin.

I frowned.

A male nurse had now joined the scene, clearly to replace the kind nurse to calm Mark down. Mark was now flexing his fists as the woman nurse strode quickly into my room. As she shut the door, she saw the small, curtainless crack and adjusted it.

"So," she began while checking monitors, "you don't really have a brother, do you?"

I couldn't help but chuckle. "No. I have a sister though. Younger."

"Look, hun, I don't mean to intrude, and I am not going to hound you for answers. But, how do I put this… you weren't attacked by no dog. I found a large scale in one of your wounds. I own some snakes and reptiles myself. Whatever this was from, was massive." She pulled a small specimen bag out of the pocket of her scrubs, pressing it into my hand. She continued as I stared at the long, thin scale, dark gray in color and keeled to a sharp point in the baggie. "I'm not sure why I did it, so let's keep this between us. When you first came in, I saw this in the wound and I pulled it out. I meant to show this to the doctors. But I ended up keeping it. I don't know anything about this. But," she gripped my hand, taking my attention away from the scale for a moment, "I do know something about love and relationships. And you shouldn't be stringing both men along like that. It's not fair."

"I . . . no. You . . . I mean . . . Edrick is really just a friend."

"Edrick?" She glanced toward the hall, but the curtain now blocked her view. "You mean Bob?" I giggled. It hurt, but it felt good. "Yeah, I had a feeling that wasn't his real name. I usually ask for ID, but with him . . ." She blushed. "He just had this way of convincing me that he cared about you, but, not in a creepy way.

"And Mark, was it?"

"He is my... boyfriend."

"You don't sound convinced." She grunted, giving me a stern look. "Or excited to see him. Has he done anything to hurt you, Brianna? Would you like for me to send him away?"

"No! He hasn't hurt me!" I blurted. "I just, dunno how I feel about him, I guess."

"Because you're falling in love with Edrick?"

"I... no, not that!" I could feel myself blushing as I said it and was suddenly grateful for the dim lights. Why was I even blushing? "He's really just a friend, and barely that."

"Uh huh. Well, it's not my job to sit here and try to tell you how to live. But just think about what I have said, will you? For their sakes?"

"Yeah, okay, thanks," I grumbled. I felt kind of irritated by the idea that she thought I was cheating on Mark with a guy like Edrick. *Then again, she didn't know the real Edrick. None of them did.* "So, when can I get out of here?"

"Oh, not for several days."

"What?"

"Sweetie, I don't know if you remember, but you were ripped from stem to stern. There is a lot of organ and tissue damage we had to work with. And significant loss of blood. Not to mention all of your broken bones. We've just started reducing your pain meds. It'll take a few more days for observations to make sure everything is healing properly and that no infection sets in. Then possibly PT and see if you can pass caring for yourself before we release you."

A medication dulled wave of panic spread through me. I sat up, suddenly realizing my mistake with a sharp intake of air and a groan. "No, I can't be here that long."

"Ah ah! Don't be sitting up like that! Now, lay back down!" The nurse scolded. Without even thinking, I had sunk back down into the slightly elevated bed. "Now. Don't worry about anything other than resting." She patted my hand. "Now, do you need anything, sweetie? Otherwise, it's lights out. The best medicine for you at the moment is sleep."

I knew it wouldn't look or sound good with Mark out there, ready to attack Edrick any second. But he had to know what was going on. "I... need to talk to him."

The nurse grinned. "Bob or Edrick?"

"Ed—" I stopped suddenly, realizing what she had just done.

"Sure, I'll tell him to come back tomorrow."

"Wait, no, it needs to be now. Just for a minute. It's important."

"Well, you should be resting. And it's after hours — "

"Please? You can time me. Literally, a minute. I promise I'll rest afterwards."

She frowned, but I knew she was too sweet hearted to deny me. She tapped her wristwatch as she moved toward the door. "Alright, I'll send *Bob* in. One minute. Don't stress yourself."

I smiled, slightly relieved.

She was careful to close the curtain as she left. I was partially relieved because I wouldn't be able to see the hurt or anger, I'm sure Mark was now wearing. But I was also curious as to what was going on. I didn't have to wait long. Rage permeated the glass and fabric barrier in a litany of swears. Grimacing, I knew I had just made the situation even more ugly. But what could I do?

I know, at least, I hadn't been prepared for Edrick to come in with a smug look on his face.

"Your boyfriend is not taking the situation well, if you were wondering."

"I literally have one minute," I interrupted with a growl. "They're making me stay here for several days."

The smug grin fell into a pinched concerned look so fast, it seemed he hadn't been grinning at all. He pulled a chair next to the bed and sat in it beside me. "That is going to be problematic."

"Yeah, that's why I figured you should know."

Edrick looked away, back at the door, lost in thought. "Even another night here is too long, dangerous. Dragon knows by now we have both been injured, and where specifically you are now. There was also the odd thing the mngwa said during the attack."

"The whattie-what now?"

"Mngwa," he repeated slowly. "The feline beast that broke through your house. He mentioned something in regard to a Shadow Man wanting you alive."

I shuddered, remembering the feel of dying, holding my own insides. "That thing that healed me… could that have been a Shadow Man?" The words I felt in my mind, more than heard, made me wonder. *Don't die. It's not time.*

Edrick seemed to ponder it for a second before slowly shaking his head. "I do not believe so. It was the perfect opportunity to take you. It would not make sense to heal you and then to let you be off on your way again. No. There are now two entities after you, I can only assume because you are the only remaining Summoner. But for what nefarious plans, I have not a clue."

I began to panic a bit, bringing another level of sharp pain to my guts. "Can't you do something? Like, heal me faster? What about that herby poultry thing you mentioned?"

He looked at me like I had said something ridiculous. "An 'herbal poultice' is not capable of treating wounds as severe as yours. And besides, I do not possess the skills for that level of magic. In any case, that amount of magic would draw too much unwanted attention. What would you have thought, before you met me, if someone had been brought back from death and was completely healed two days later?"

"I . . . died?" I knew in a way I had. But to hear it…

The weak will die! The weak will die!

"If only you were trained . . . a carbuncle would work—"

"Edrick, did I really die?"

73

His eyes focused on me again. "I will do what I can. But first, I have to get my sword and your staff. The illusion I put around them should be disappearing right about now."

"Edrick, I'm serious — "

The nurse poked her head in. "One minute. Time to go."

Edrick rose and gave me a nod. "Brianna, yes. You died. But you are alive now. Now, rest. I will be back, I swear." He walked past the nurse, giving her a smile I had never seen before. It was baffling. Personal. Alluring. "Thank you, ma'am," he said to the nurse. He paused, taking one of her hands and squeezing it gently. "Please take great care of my friend, Brianna."

She blushed, and the slight wobble I saw made me wonder if she was swooning. "She will want for nothing, sweetie." She watched him leave for a few good seconds before shaking her head. For a moment, she looked at me, confusion in her eyes. As quickly as it had come on, it left. "Okay, young lady. Time for you to hold up your end of the deal." She clicked the room lights off, leaving me alone in the dim silence.

I closed my eyes, tried to fall asleep. Each time my body fell into the gentleness of the pain meds, the panic would rise in my throat.

The weak will die! The weak will die!

Did that mean... me?

Did that mean I was now... reborn?

CHAPTER 9

Burning. Suffocating. The thick pain of panic, leaden adrenaline. Frozen in place, dying to run. Legs wouldn't — couldn't — move. Pain so great, it hurt less to die…

The first thing were the blue eyes. Cold. Hard. Yet they felt like a foundation. My eyes felt cold, wet, and I could feel tears drying on my cheeks.

I opened my mouth to scream, but something warm and heavy held my lips in place, muffling me.

The eyes moved back a bit, revealing a face I knew. Edrick looked at me hard and shook his head. It was his hand over my mouth.

I nodded before moving my head to the side, drawing in a quiet gulp of air.

Dragon, I mouthed the word. When I was a kid, I used to love dragons. Faries. Unicorns. All of those fun, fantasy things pretty much all kids were into at some point. But now, now these things filled me with dread. No, worse. Soul gripping fear.

And Dragon. Dragon I now feared the most.

Somehow, Edrick's face grew even more tense, harder. He returned the nod, then reached over to the side. Quickly, he tossed a bundle of my clothes onto the bed beside me, leaving the staff resting against the sliding bed bar.

I tried to sit up. My body exploded with pains and aches so deep, I could only get my head, shoulders, and arms off the bed.

Realizing I couldn't get up on my own, Edrick frowned. Hesitantly, he moved beside me, moving his hand down to the middle of my back. Goosebumps popped up on my arms as I felt a shiver go up my neck. But before I could reflect on it further, I felt him guide me up into a fully seated position.

Fully seated, I winced, a wave of vertigo crashing over me. Bile filled my throat and my mouth filled with warm saliva. I shook my head violently. I couldn't do this!

"Hurry, or worse will befall all those here," he whispered in my ear. "Find your strength, Summoner!"

I wanted to say, *go fuck yourself, I don't care*. I wanted to lay back down. His hand though remained firmly pressed against my back. Supporting me. Yet warning me of the urgency. My mindset seemed to change in an instant.

Once again, I looked to him as a foundation. I could do this.

Gritting my teeth and thankful for the darkness, I swung my legs over the side of the bed, wadding the thin blankets up beside me. Thankfully, I was no longer hooked up to anything. Even so, many sensations crawled across my belly. Pulling, burning pain. Severe itching. And inside, a deeper, throbbing ache. My belly also felt swollen.

Gingerly, I grabbed my shirt and bra, waiting. It took Edrick a long moment before his eyes widened with realization, and with a blush, he turned away.

I had never taken so long to dress in my life. And the most painful thing I can remember ever having to do to myself. Edrick got up and stood by the door, looking through a crack in the curtain for, I assumed, any incoming nurses. After several minutes however, when he realized my struggles, he hurried over and helped pull the sweater down snug to my waist. Tears were streaming from my eyes from the pain of the effort. Try as he might, I caught him staring at my bandages before the sweater covered them.

He grabbed my arm with one hand and started to pull me up when I gripped him suddenly with my other hand. "I can't," I muttered. My skin was covered in gooseflesh from the discomfort of the bruises and wounds. Sweat had started forming across my brow, making the cool room feel even colder. All of my muscles began twitching and pulling in protest. Black circles started to fill my vision as I moaned in agony, clenching my teeth to keep myself from crying out.

Edrick looked at me again, this time his eyes filled with apathy. It startled me. "I know." Glancing back towards the door, he grabbed me firmly by both wrists. "I am sorry. But it must be done."

In one sudden motion, he pulled me up off the bed and toward him, up to my feet. I fell against him, weakly. My face fell into his chest and I began to cry. He held me tightly, probably to keep my cries from being heard. In between sobs, I could smell his shirt. It was gloriously distracting.

Mark's smell.

But it wasn't Mark.

And somehow, that felt even better.

Steeling myself, I grabbed hold of his arms and lifted myself away from him with a sniffle and a deep breath.

Edrick looked down at me. Not out of happiness. Or frustration. But pride.

No one had ever looked at me that way before.

"I knew you could," he reassured me, smiling. He grabbed the staff behind me and pressed it into my left hand. "You will get better, Brianna. And I will get you somewhere safe. But we need to get out of here first."

Already exhausted, I nodded. Adjusting my grip on the staff, I took my first step.

You couldn't call it hobbling. It was more like the slow lumbering of someone at Death's Door. By the time I made it to the entryway, my body trembled fiercely. My clothes felt damp with sweat, and my head pounded. Edrick kept tugging me, supporting most of my weight with one of his arms around me. He cracked open the door and looked out. I now leaned heavily against him and could see into the hallway.

To the left stood a nurse's station. Two nurses were manning the floor, both young looking and wearing matching scrubs with elegant leaf designs. The farthest nurse had her back to me, looking at a computer screen. She looked to be shopping online, running her fingers through a patch of blonde hair as if grooming herself. The other nurse sat turned most of the way from us, light brown hair done up in an elegant bun, flipping through a magazine with gorgeously manicured nails. Other than the bright lights over the desk, the rest of the lights in the hallway were dimmed so as not to disturb the patients.

Edrick's face tightened as he slipped out the door. He pressed himself to the right of the wall, keeping his eyes on the nurse's station. One hand rested on the pommel of his sword, the other gripping my arm almost too tightly.

I wrapped my arm around the staff, pinning it tight to my chest. Leaning against the cool, tiled wall allowed me to rest most of my weight and slide. My heart pounded even faster now, the bile in my throat making it hard to breathe. I know Edrick wanted me to be strong, move faster, but I didn't think I was capable of going on much longer. Did he even have any idea how much pain I was in?

We hadn't moved more than ten feet from the exit when my knees suddenly buckled. There had been no warning, nothing I could have done to stop it. I fell to the floor in an exhausted heap, the staff clattering, obscenely loud, from my hands to the tiles. I heaved so hard on impact, it felt like my guts were trying to find a new way out. I barely gasped for breath when another wave hit, forcing my stomach to act as if sucker punching my spine. I reached out with a hand, gripping the staff as if that would somehow help. Actually, clinging to it tightly kind of did.

Startled out of their bored daze, the two nurses both yelped and jumped to their feet. Another wave of nausea forced my eyes down. Standing over me, Edrick said something under his breath, inaudible over the sound of sneakers running down the hall. My ears started ringing, and I couldn't hear anything over my own hurling.

A dark shadow fell across me seconds before an angry shout. Something collapsed in front of me, splashing some of my vomit back into my face. I screamed, too weak to back away.

The blonde nurse's eye remained open, glazed over. Blood leaked on the floor beneath her face. Or what was left of it. It had been laid open, a bloody broken mess. Crushed bone shone through bloody, pulpy skin. The other eye stared at a different angle, bulging from the socket.

A commotion played out above me. I couldn't tear my eyes away until the second nurse landed partially on the first.

"What the fu—"

The wind was knocked from me before I could finish. I didn't even react as Edrick hauled me up with one hand, the other wrapped around the grip of his sword. I barely clung to the staff which felt heavier than it was.

The violent motion however made me puke again, this time all over Edrick's shoulder. There thankfully wasn't much left in me. He didn't even seem to flinch.

Somewhere, an alarm had started up. Slow, red-flashing lights kicked on, bathing the hallways in bright, flashing lights.

Too many stimuli forced me to squeeze my eyes shut. My torso bounced painfully on Edrick as he ran through the hospital. I tried to tell him to stop, that I couldn't take anymore. It took all I had to hold onto the staff, to keep breathing. Tears fell from my eyes. Behind my lids, all I could see were the destroyed faces of the two nurses. *Why did he kill them?*

The world suddenly halted and I cried out in pain. Edrick thankfully held onto me tightly enough that if he hadn't, I would have fallen.

"Freeze!" shouted a man's voice. "Put the sword and the girl down!"

Edrick snarled, and I could feel his grip on me tighten. "Sir, please, out of my way. You do not understand what is going to happen."

Happen?

I heard more footsteps rapidly approaching, taking place next to what I assumed was the first cop or security guard. I was facing backwards, unable to see what was actually going on. "Put her down," a second voice rang clear, but firm, "or I will be forced to shoot."

I assumed by their willingness to shoot that we were being targeted by tasers. I can't imagine they would have bullets flying around a hospital, or even be willing to hit the victim, me, in order to get the kidnapper, Edrick. At least, I hoped that was what they were doing. Not that I really wanted to be tased. In my condition, I imagined I would probably die.

Beneath my own chest, I felt Edrick's wildly pounding heart skip a beat. He was panicking. Would he know what tasers were? Or did he think they were guns? Before I could say anything though, he whispered, "Hang on, this is about to get ugly."

Behind me, a terrific crashing sound happened. Several screams and cries of surprise erupted, and I recognized the voices of the two officers. Edrick fell to his right side, holding me too tight. The impact jarred me hard, and I bit my tongue, not prepared for what happened. I ended up on top of Edrick, screaming in agony. Whatever had been holding my wounds closed ripped open. Warm, wet sensations slowly began to creep along my stomach.

Edrick rolled me off of him with a firm shove. Freed, I balled myself up, trying to protect my stomach as I sort of half rolled and half flopped under some chairs of the waiting room. Through tears of pain, I recognized the waiting room of the local hospital.

Chaos had ensued throughout. Screaming and shouting paled in comparison to the animal grunts and screeches. Things fell and clattered, adding to the cacophony.

Edrick's face appeared, blurry. Grabbing one of my hands, tightly, he forced the staff into my palm, closing my grip around it tightly with his own. What I could see of his face seemed tense, though his eyes stood wide open, his lips a thin, tight line. Blood smeared one cheek, though there were no wounds. "Stay down. Stay back. No magic unless as a last resort. And if you can, run!"

I didn't have the strength to reply. I was barely able to keep my eyes open as he climbed to his feet and rushed into the fray.

Most of my view consisted of pairs of legs scurrying about. Ten or so feet away, a young man fell to the floor, unmoving. Sounds of confusion and cries of pain bombarded my ears.

And I heard a howl. And eerie, snarling howl almost too painful to hear.

Wincing and trembling, I pulled myself toward the edge of the chairs so I could see more.

A large beast thrashed about, shaking its massive head in a brownish blur. Another body fell to the floor. Without wasting a second, the monster leapt toward another victim, an older woman, already injured. The cops and hospital security stood in a line, blocking the creature's ingress. Around their feet lay spent tasers. They bore pistols now and as one, started firing.

Bullets slammed into the monster and he shook the woman like a lifeless ragdoll. No wounds or blood appeared on its thick hide.

A sharp whistle cut through the air, catching both the attention of the police and guards, who momentarily stopped shooting the beast. Now, I was able to get a good look at it.

Nearly seven feet long, and three feet high at the shoulder, the beast had thick, dark brown flesh with sparse patches of bristle. A long line of wicked black spikes ran from its stout, short muzzle to the tip of its short, thick tail. It had a bulldog-like face filled with wicked, protruding fangs. Tusks curved down and outward from its lower jaw. Horns protruded from the sides of its face. Large, yellow eyes stared out from beneath a heavy brow. It took two steps toward Edrick on its short, muscular legs. I could hear the clacking of its claws against the tiled floor.

Edrick stood alone facing it. His sweater was torn, revealing his still damaged leathers beneath. The streak of blood remained on his left cheek, a larger, darker stain over his shoulder and down to the front of the sweater. His hair had come loose from the leather strip. In his hands, unwavering, he bared his long sword. Reddish runes began to glow down the center of the blade as his lips moved with quick, silent words.

The beast barked and leapt.

Edrick grunted as he slashed at the monster. The boar looking creature side-stepped with an agility it didn't look to possess. Around them, the sound of gunfire resumed.

"Stop!" I tried to shout. The way the authorities shot blindly, some trembling, they were likely to hit Edrick and not the beast!

The creature launched into a savage attack. It didn't react as bullets slammed harmlessly into its sides, but it darted towards Edrick, evading the sword. With a sudden, sharp clang of teeth on metal, it wrapped its muzzle around the blade. The unexpected maneuver pulled Edrick toward the ground. The monster shook its head violently, as it had with the others, trying to rip the sword from the Guardian's grip. Edrick grimaced, face red with strain as he scrambled to stay on his feet. His arms twisted in various directions, his knuckles turning white from his grip as he tried to wrest the blade from the monster's mouth.

The monster snarled, snapping its head sharply to one side, trying to tear Edrick's hold. With its closest paw, it began swatting at Edrick. Thankfully Edrick stood outside its short reach. Like cat's claws, it managed to snag the fabric of nearby chairs. Cushions ripped, sending plumes of stuff, as if made of paper, into the air and on the floor.

With a pained grunt, Edrick tore the sword loose. The maneuver cut a long gash in the side of the creatures' mouth. The beast howled in pain. Red, bloodshot anger laced its now narrowed eyes, snarling at its opponent.

The cops and guards finally paused their firing, or they had run out of bullets. Three of them had begun throwing directions at the others and pointing. I couldn't hear anything but ringing after all the firing and howling.

Edrick's face tightened and twisted in pain and focus. I suddenly noticed the scratch marks across his left shin, barely bleeding, but the denim cloth was in tatters. Scratches also stood out on one wrist. I wondered when that had happened as the lightheadedness threatened to take my consciousness.

The weak die, the strong reborn, I could hear through the ringing. *You will be the redeemer.*

"Run!" I heard someone shout, muffled by the distance and ringing.

I know I should have listened to Edrick. I wanted nothing more than to run. A hot rage filled me, as I stared at the unmoving bodies on the floor. People dying, again. Not just Kara. People who had no choice getting caught up in all of this.

I had to help. Had to stop running!

If there was only one thing I seemed to be good at, it was summoning up a manticore.

Darkness threatened my eyes and mind. The pain was getting worse, but I wanted, no, *needed* to help. Wanted...

I gripped the staff tighter in my hand. I tried to move myself out from under the chair, onto my hands and knees, but the pain was too great. I looked down and saw blood — my blood— on the floor. Would I even be able to summon a manticore, let alone control it? The memory of the pain, confusion, that both the previous ones felt made me faulter.

In the distance, the beast swiped again at Edrick. He hopped backwards. His feet landed on something, rolling, throwing him off balance.

Falling!

The swimming sensation filled my head again as I clutched the staff tightly in both hands, resting my chest on it. I had to do it. The sensation flooded my mind. The feel of another. One that was, but wasn't mine...

The nausea rolled up fast. I hadn't been expecting that. The pain of dry heaving with damaged guts only enhanced the discomfort and disassociation. I gasped for air, only to find myself fighting against my reactions.

A new sound filled the air. Like the screeching of a giant hawk, but larger, deeper. The tall, open lobby of the hospital was filled with a nearly imperceptible flash, replaced by a large, golden bird. The body stretched as long as a man, yet its wings filled a great portion of the room. Red-gold eyes peered down at the pig-creature. It hissed, a crest of feathers on its head flattening.

It was not a manticore.

The four-legged beast attacked first. It jumped at the bird, barking and snarling, Edrick suddenly forgotten. The bird shrieked, wheeling backward.

It was the opportunity Edrick was looking for, as he clambered back to his feet.

In a flash, he lunged, sword first, at the beast. I could see the tip of the sword hesitate for the briefest moment in time as it connected with the bullet-tough hide, in between its ribcage. Then, the skin caved in. Edrick grunted as he shoved all his weight behind the thrust, driving the sword as deep as he could.

The beast howled in pain, whirling toward Edrick. The man tried to step back, but the sword held firm. The monster's motion turned the sword away from him, ripping the hilt from his grip.

The bird launched itself, feet first, at the monster. Golden, sharp talons latched themselves onto the beasts' back. Terrible sounds erupted from both as blood and golden feathers flew in all directions.

The vertigo became too much for me. With a groan, I fell to my side and closed my eyes.

CHAPTER 10

Warm tendrils, like lying in the sun, caressed my skin. The coziness of snuggling into my most comfortable blanket. Rich aromas of home and comfort filling the nose. I felt safe. Whole. I cracked my eyes open, bathing in golden light. For a moment, my body tensed, ready for the pain, the burning, that would come from such brilliance. Yet there was none.

It felt... glorious.

I reached out to touch the light, to feel with skin the marvel before me. The light quickly faded. Instead, Edrick filled my vision once again.

I groaned as I pushed myself back up. But not out of pain or discomfort. From disappointment.

Edrick's face appeared paled, weary. His wide, stone-blue eyes stared at me, his mouth slightly agape. It wasn't my face he was looking at though. His eyes were focused farther down.

I followed his gaze, feeling a cool breeze on my skin. I grabbed at my shirt and yanked it down. "Hey!"

His eyes met mine as a blush crept up the side of his neck and into his cheeks. "I-I am sorry. It is not... your wounds..."

I sat up farther against a cold wood wall, pulling the hem of my sweater up to just below my chest. I hadn't seen the wounds yet, not that I had been in the hospital and conscious long enough to do so. But now, there was nothing to see. Where I had felt incredible pain before, where blood stains still streaked some of my skin, was nothing. Not even the holes of staples or stitches. Next to me lay a pile of gauze wraps and bandages, all covered with old, dried blood. Edrick must have taken them off, looking to tend to my wounds.

I looked up at Edrick, my own face I'm sure, filled with shock and awe. "How? What happened?"

He shook his head, sitting back on his heels. "It was the alicanto you summoned. It fought the hodag. I do not know — "

"The what to fight the what?"

"The hodag. The dog-pig monster. With the teeth and spines. Dragon must have sent it to hunt you out. They are one of the best blood trackers in the world. It must have followed your scent to the hospital."

"Hodag," I repeated softly. "And the other creature? The ali-co-whatever — "

"Alicanto," he gently corrected. "Insatiable creatures that feed on silver and gold. They have some healing abilities. But… nothing like this. And it fought like an eagle, light. Quick. It must have taken your direction." He shook his head again, his brown knitted in thought. "But you did not know what that was? And it was the third time you have summoned a powerful creature, again when your life was most threatened."

"I don't know," was all I could think to say. That's when I really noticed our surroundings. Dark. Cold. "Where are we? This… this isn't the hospital."

"No. You passed out. While the alicanto was finishing off the hodag, I dragged you out. Those lawmen who were firing on us scattered, calling for help. As we left, I could hear sirens approaching. I took us into the woods, and finally came up to this old shed."

And boy was it old! I used to play in sheds like these with my friends when we were in elementary school. A dilapidated tool and storage shed. Countless others, similar to this one, laid scattered throughout the middle of old apple orchards. They were common places for teens to get high or get laid in. The wood walls warped from exposure to time and the elements, rotting from decades of neglect. The tin roof appeared rusted and pitted; whole sections completely rotted out. Ancient nail holes, the nails themselves long gone, left rotted gaps in the metal the size of a finger. Long tracks of low sunlight stabbed into the darker reaches of the shack. Like a swarm of fruit flies, dust motes and possibly pollen, hell, maybe even mold spores, drifted in and out of the beams. If it were warmer out, the place would have been crawling with all sorts of disgusting bugs.

Filthy, jagged edged and splintered walls somewhat protected the disgusting insides; old butts and stubs, dirt, animal droppings, mold, and god-only-knows what else. And worse, it was damp and cold.

Now that I wasn't caught in the throes of bodily pain and imminent danger, I felt chilled to the bone. I began to shiver, tucking my hands under my armpits for warmth. The sweater was more decorative than useful. And even worse than the cold, the gnawing pangs of hunger. "I'm so hungry," I murmured, my teeth beginning to chatter. "And cold. But mostly hungry."

Edrick frowned. "Right. It has been a while since you have eaten." He looked around, as if to find inspiration in the shitty shack. "It could take a while, but I could hunt something down—"

"No!" I shouted. The thought of him hacking a deer or bunny to bits—

The memory struck me hard, forcing a gasp from my lips. "You-you killed those nurses, didn't you?"

Adjusting the old log he currently used as a seat, Edrick paused. "Killed nurses? I… ah, no, those were not nurses."

"Uh, the hell they weren't," I spat. A shudder ran through me, remembering their once beautiful, now crushed faces. "You killed humans—"

"Those two were not humans," he interrupted. "They were tanuki."

I buried my head in my hands. "Is everything not as it seems?"

"Only here," Edrick replied, not that I was looking for an answer. "Female Tanuki hide themselves as human females. Generally, they are harmless. But there are too many coincidences happening around you, it seems. I am not willing to risk anything. Who knows who they are working with, why they were keeping an eye on you, why they got up to stop us." He shook his head. "Something extremely dangerous is going on, Brianna. I came here in search of the Lyndheart, and instead, find you being pursued by two forces, one of which I believe is new to the Order's knowledge. There has not been this much activity in hundreds of years."

I shook my head. "I'm so cold." From the angle of the sun I could tell it was nearly nighttime.

"We cannot build a fire, I am sorry."

I moved to stand up, realizing I no longer hurt, anywhere. Now, I was just freezing. "Well, then, I need to get back home. Get something warm—"

Edrick reached out and grabbed my elbow tightly. "Brianna, you cannot go home. I told you, I will need to get you into hiding, somewhere. Some place where Dragon and this Shadow Man cannot easily get you."

"If we can't have a fire, I need clothes. And food! I didn't go through everything the past several…" I paused. Holy crap, how long had it been now? I wanted to say days, but it might actually have been weeks. *Was this going to be my new life, my new normal? Running, hiding, being hunted, one incident after another?* "I'm not going to die of hypothermia." I paused. "Maybe… maybe we can go to one of my friend's houses."

"No," he snapped, pulling on my elbow. I dropped back down against the wall, hugging myself. I felt super pissed off. Like, about ready to summon a manticore for him to deal with so I could go get some clothes and food pissed. Almost immediately, I realized how horrible an idea that was. To throw a living being at him, ripped from its home, just to fill some need for comforts.

Edrick continued, but none of it made me feel any better. "You cannot go back to your apartment. Possibly never again. Dragon is after you, and I still do not know why. He has enough power to bring beasts from the Chaos Realm over himself. I do not believe being a Summoner is enough to warrant him putting so many powerful beasts out to find and take you. I am not certain, either, that he would rather see you dead."

I wrapped my arms around myself again and shivered slightly. "So, what does that mean?"

"It means you cannot go to those places you used to frequent. You cannot go anywhere public where you will be recognized."

"Only a handful of people know me in this town. How would anyone recognize me?"

Edrick grew uncomfortable. "Not long after we escaped the hospital, I went back to make sure we were not being followed, to cover any trace of where we went such as blood or scent. People on the street were talking about you, by name. I listened to some of the conversations, and it seems that law enforcement is looking for you and a 'strange man' who appears armed and dangerous." He couldn't seem to help himself as he turned towards me with a grin.

I didn't find the humor in it. *Everyone is looking for me,* was all I could think. "But why should I care," I muttered more to myself than him "I didn't do anything wrong. Why should I be afraid—"

87

"You are correct. You did nothing wrong," Edrick replied. "Yet the community is being led to believe I... kidnapped you. Now that Dragon has imagery of you and especially of myself, he can have agents in the human world be on the lookout. He has made me sound terribly dangerous, and you in mortal danger. Everyone will be talking; everyone will be looking. Now all he needs to do is sit back and wait for the rest of the world to find you. After the injuries you sustained a few days ago, after the fighting in the hospital, what do you think they will do once someone recognizes you?"

I wanted to cry. All I wanted to do was go home. "It's not fair," I barely said, my throat choked up with a lump. "I'm penniless, now on the run. And I can't go to anyone for help." I could feel my chest tightening up again. Great, because I needed a full-on anxiety attack at the moment. "I can't do this. I can't do this."

Edrick moved in front of me, putting both of his hands on my shoulder. He was so calm, yet how could he be? "It will be okay, I promise you," he spoke softly, his eyes keeping mine locked with his. "I promise you will be safe, that I will protect you. But you will have to listen to me. You have to follow everything I say, even if it does not make sense, alright?"

I looked away.

After a few seconds, he stood up. "I am going to find you some food, maybe something warmer." He paused before walking out of the shack. I think he was waiting for me to respond, for affirmation that I was going to do what he said.

Did I have a choice? I now had nothing left.

Nothing.

I turned away from him so he couldn't see the tears coming from my eyes.

"I will be back shortly. Stay here."

I must have fallen asleep. The next thing I knew, I was awake, shivering. Hunger gnawed at my guts that while healed, still ached in need of food. The sunlight faded faster as clouds rolled in, bringing darkness, and falling temperatures.

Edrick hadn't returned.

The clouds obscured any light from the moon or stars. I had nothing on me that I could use as a light source.

I was beyond cold. I was freezing. Not freezing cold. Like, about to die from hypothermia cold. One part of me wanted to lie here and just keep waiting. Curl into a ball, don't leave the warm spot I had made on the ground. The other part of me had been in full-blown panic mode. What could be taking Edrick so long? What if he had been noticed and arrested? What if some monster from the Chaos Realm found him and managed to kill him?

How long could I wait here in the dark and cold, not knowing?

Stiffly, I climbed to my feet. I had to risk it. I had to find food, something warm, or better shelter. Even if it meant someone noticed me, which I still found doubtful.

I found myself walking for several minutes, a light snow lazily falling before I realized I hadn't grabbed the staff! I turned around, tried to walk back in the dark. I literally couldn't see anything more than a foot or so in front of me. Walking helped warm me up a little, and I began to hike faster. I should have reached the shed by now. Had I wandered just far enough to miss it? Had I not walked far enough?

I did something stupid, realizing it all too late. I stopped. Turned. Listened, while searching in the dark for anything. The snow now dusted the ground, wet flakes clinging to my face, cold. I had to keep walking. Forget the staff! If I couldn't find my way through the ancient orchard, neither could anyone else. And I would notice a flashlight before anyone noticed me.

I felt like I walked a long time, bare hands tucked under my arm pits, walking as quickly as I could without tripping. Fallen trees and rotting branches littered the once manicured orchard. Once groomed lanes of grass had been overcome by wild rose bushes, scrub bushes, tall clumps of grass and goldenrod which still stood taller than me and brown this late into the year. Here and there, copse of poplar and white birch reclaimed the land. There were many places like this in town, which was well known for its apple orchards and various businesses with specialty apple products. Most orchards remained new and well kept. Yet numerous farms over its two-hundred-year history had been made and abandoned. Many times, those properties had remained wild, leaving ancient sheds like the one Edrick had found, and great spots for kids to camp in the summer without being too far from home. The farther I walked and reminisced, the less scary the night became. I even smiled some, remembering how my younger sister, Elizabeth, and I had camped such places numerous times. The farther I walked, the more a dream the past week—two weeks? Who knew! —seemed.

"Lost, are ye?"

I yelped, whirling around. "Who are you?"

"Not lost," the feminine voice dripped, closer this time.

I turned again, still unable to see a body with the voice. "I-I have a gun!" I couldn't think of what else to say.

The voice laughed. "No, you don't, little Summoner."

I swallowed hard. Was it human? It knew I didn't have a weapon. Knew what I was.

Idiot!

"Don't worry your pretty little head," the voice seemed to purr near my ear. "I'm not here to harm you. I could have done that hours ago while you were sleeping."

"Who—"

Something soft and warm brushed against my hand. I started to snatch my hand back, but the woman grabbed it before I could, holding tightly. "Let's walk, shall we?"

I didn't have a choice. The woman seemed to coalesce out of the darkness. Her warm hand slid into my arm, linking us at the elbows. She walked. I followed alongside.

I couldn't make out much in the darkness. She seemed a bit taller than me. Thin, and much more buxom. A dark hood and cape covered most her body except for her face, neck, and chest that seemed to glow in the darkness. The dress she wore appeared so low cut, it didn't seem practical at all for winter wear, exposing way more of her chest than I would have dared. The cowl covered all but several long locks of dark hair, and from what I could see, her petite nose, high cheeks, and delicate features shone like an antique china doll.

I found myself pressing into her body as we walked through the woods. I should have been scared. Or at least curious. But a soothing calm had fallen over me. I was no longer alone. This woman, with her cozy soft cloak and gloves, would keep me warm. She would show me the way.

"Tis my luck you give up too easily," she spoke after several minutes. That is when I noticed an accent to her voice like nothing I had ever heard before. "No surprise you didn't listen to my dear Aedrick." She giggled. "He was never good with the ladies though, poor thing."

"Who are you?" I struggled to ask. Deep within, I knew I wanted to know, yet a greater part of me almost didn't care.

"You, may address me as Miss Laura-Lei, my pet," she replied, patting the top of my hand. "Now, go ahead. I know you are absolutely burning to ask. And maybe, I will tell you."

I opened my mouth, a dozen questions all at once at the tip of my tongue, but only one made it out. "Where are we going?"

Laura-Lei giggled again. "That's a surprise, pet." She turned her head, and even without light, I could see her dark brown eyes flecked with amber. "Ah, do not forget your manners, little one."

"Yes, Miss Laura-Lei," I found myself replying.

Laura-Lei remained silent. I was still burning with questions. How had she found me? How did she know I was a Summoner? Yet it seemed impossible to ask. Just as impossible it was for me to slow down. Fatigue from the cold and lack of food, and now thirst, was starting to wear on me. I needed a break. Yet I couldn't find a way to communicate this to the strange woman. And I couldn't slow down if I tried. My legs matched her stride step-by-step. Panic made my mind race. Was she going to kill me, another monster of the Chaos Realm I now foolishly followed? Yet every time I tried to clear my mind, to feel hers out, there was nothing there.

Could she be another Guardian?

I remembered Edrick telling me that all Summoners and Guardians were male. But if I somehow managed to be a female Summoner, could it be possible? Maybe she was a female Guardian he didn't know about.

I walked quietly for maybe fifteen minutes, led by Laura-Lei with our elbows still linked, when I heard a familiar sound, loud in the dark. The hissing scrape of a sword being drawn.

"Release her. Now!"

I could hear the fluttering in Laura-Lei's voice as she spoke, though not at all in fear. "I'd nearly forgotten the sound of your sweet voice, dear boy!"

"I will not ask again, sorceress!"

"Or what? You'll cut me down in some heroic maneuver?" I could hear her smirking. "You couldn't then to save your own father, little Guardian. I doubt you could do more now."

I heard the whistling of the sword cutting through the night before I saw the flash of the blade. Laura-Lei barely moved. The arm not wrapped around mine rose, and she held out a finger. From this distance, I could see her finger touching the point of the blade. "Such poor manners, striking at an unarmed lady." She tsked. When neither moved for a minute, she sighed. "Fine," she muttered, dropping her hand. At the same time, I felt her warm arm unwind from my own. "Scurry to your little Guardian, pet."

"Yes, Miss Laura-Lei," I found myself saying without even thinking as I started walking ahead.

"Let her go, completely."

"Oh, and where is the fun in that?"

I could now feel a strong hand, Edrick's, gripping my arm, hard. He pulled me behind him, and I thought I could feel him trembling. "Brianna are you harmed?" he asked quietly.

"Harmed? I found your little pet wandering the woods without even a weapon," Laura-Lei butted in, sounding hurt. "I was keeping the poor thing company. Wasn't I?"

"Yes—"

"Laura-Lei!"

"Fine!" she spat.

Suddenly, I found myself freezing again. I gripped Edrick's arms, but even the coat he now wore felt cold in my hands. My teeth began to chatter. "Wh-wh-what's going on?"

"Shall I tell her?" I could hear the grin in her voice.

"Why are you here?" he ignored her.

The strange woman laughed quietly to herself, before saying something in a language I'd never heard before. Beneath my hands, I felt Edrick flinch. He replied in the same sounding tongue, though his words came slow, menacing. I began shaking so hard now, I felt sick. "Edrick—"

Laura-Lei said something again in the foreign language before laughing.

Edrick reached out and grabbed me with one arm as I suddenly felt my legs give out. Tremors ripped through my body, while at the same time, making all my limbs feel like jelly. Held tight in one arm, I could feel Edrick trembling, his right hand still holding Laura-Lei at sword's length. "And there it is, my pet. I don't know who placed it on you, but it is the mark of Dragon. That is how he is tracking you."

The tremors began to quiet, leaving me gasping for air. I couldn't think more than simple thoughts. Cold. Hunger. My entire body felt wrong. And now, the one person who had been my only mountain for weeks, was crumbling himself.

"Tell your Guardian, pet. How do you feel?"

"Something is wrong with me," I found my lips barely able to murmur. I scarcely had the strength to breathe. How was I able to talk at all? Nausea tore at me, yet my stomach was so empty, all it caused was extreme discomfort. "Miss Laura-Lei, I'm cold, hungry, and in pain."

"You are not going to take her," Edrick snarled. "Not even God knows what you will use her for."

"Likely the same reason you are using her," the woman scoffed. "To draw out Dragon himself, and to find the Lyndheart. Except, I'll let her go when I'm done with her, not—"

Edrick's voice drowned out whatever Laura-Lei had been ready to say as he hollered in the foreign language.

I hadn't seen her move. From Edrick's reaction, he hadn't either. His grip on me tightened, drawing my still limp body tighter to his chest. Yet I could feel his entire body stiffen, frightened. The sound of his sword clattering to the ground beneath us made my heart freeze. Even from this close, I could make out Laura-Lei's whispers in his ear. "Don't you *ever* threaten me again, *boy*. I, too, have learned a few tricks over the centuries." I could see upward enough to spot the glint of a small blade, barely the size of a steak knife but wider. She held it steady in the palm of her gloved hand, its sharp edge pushing the boundaries of skin at the side of Edrick's neck. "Whatever dark purpose I serve is my own, and not nearly as cold hearted as your own ends." She paused, and I could feel Edrick's heart race, his breath held.

"Hmm, heart," Laura-Lei said softly, running the blade from Edrick's neck slowly down his chest. He now shuddered, and I could just make out her winking at me. "With power like this, the three of us—"

"No," Edrick interrupted, his voice somewhat breathless. "Laura-Lei, please."

93

Time stretched for a moment. I had no idea what was going on, except that this woman, this *human* woman scared Edrick more than anything else had during our time together so far. That terrified me. What did she mean to him, and why did he fear her in a way he hadn't been afraid of any of the monsters? The need to ask burned inside of me, yet I still couldn't seem to find a way to talk or ask on my own. I could barely think.

Laura-Lei finally sighed as if she were bored. As quick as the knife in her hand had appeared, it was gone. She stepped away from the two of us, brushing invisible wrinkles from the front of her dress. I say invisible because a dress that form fitting couldn't possibly hold a wrinkle. "Well, then, my love, it looks like you will keep your heart for the time being. I can wait," she paused, and for the first time, I saw a darkness to her face, her eyes. "But not forever." She turned and began to walk away. "Oh, and pet, this time you are released, completely." I could hardly make out the flourish of one hand over her head as she continued into the black of night. "And Dragon's tracer is gone from you. You can thank me next time we meet. See you around, Aedrick."

Edrick bent down slowly and with his free hand, picked up his sword, and sheathed it. I felt… strange, didn't quite fit, but no better words came to mind. Different. Hollow. Definitely confused, as Edrick then used his other hand to scoop me up. Without a word, he carried me back to the shed.

CHAPTER 11

The journey back to the shed took much less time than it had while wandering alone in the darkness. I didn't speak, too tired and too anxious to talk. Instead, I tried to figure out why Laura-Lei scared Edrick so much. In the week or so I had known him, I had never seen him drop his sword, let alone slip his grip on it. Never saw him as vulnerable as I had tonight. All this time, to me at least, he had been a strange, ancient hero, weathering both time and monsters on some weird quest to keep the world safe. Someone like that had to be made of stone.

What I saw tonight was a man. A human man. With fears, weaknesses. Someone who wasn't beneath begging.

Laura-Lei. Please.

I still didn't know what to think or say once he set me down inside. Shivering, I watched as he shrugged off the large felt coat he wore and draped it around me like a blanket. The warmth oozed into my icy skin, soothing the ache of my cold-weary muscles.

"You left." It wasn't a question. "I told you not to leave, that I would be back."

"I didn't know," I finally managed to mutter, pulling the edges of the coat tighter around me.

"I told you I would be back. Did you not believe me?" He stood hoovering over me. Thankfully, I couldn't make out his expression in the dark from this distance.

"Do you know how alone and cold and hungry I was?" I shot back before thinking. "You have no idea what it's like, all of this, for me! I don't know what is going to happen to me, from one minute to the next."

"I left you here, to stay safe," Edrick replied. He sounded tired, not himself. "There was a ward in place, hiding this and you. Because of your leaving, it broke. Dragon's or the Shadow Man's minions could have found you."

"She knew where I was, the whole time," I said. I knew I should have just shut up and gotten some sleep. But I now felt that special kind of tired where you could muster up a fight out of nothing. And damnit! I wanted to know what was going on! "Laura-Lei. She said she could have killed me at any time. Who the fuck was she, anyway?"

"No one."

"Bullshit," I snorted. "She seemed to know you really well."

I heard more than saw him sit with a heavy sigh. "Please, Brianna—"

"Yeah, I know, don't swear."

"No, that is not... I..." Edrick faltered.

Silence filled the small shed. "I-I'm sorry." *Or what? You'll cut me down in some heroic maneuver? You couldn't then to save your own father, little Guardian. I doubt you could do more now.* "She... she killed your father, didn't she?"

Despite the darkness, I could see Edrick drop his head to his chest. "No. I did."

"I... I'm sorry," I stammered, apologizing again. "I... I shouldn't have asked."

"But you did." Exhaling loudly, he crossed his arms. He looked smaller, huddled in the dark. "I promised you I would not lie. But I do not think I can tell you... the whole truth."

"Like, why you killed your father?"

"Brianna, in the short time I have known you, you are singularly brave, foolish, and weak. You come close to the point of transformation, where the bravery could overcome your weakness, yet you consistently give up."

"I... I'm sorry. I didn't mean—"

He shook his head, stopping me. "No. You do not. And therein lies the issue. I cannot protect you if you choose not to be saved. And that is my fault."

"Edrick, please stop. I'm sorry!"

"You have sidetracked me," he continued. "I came across you in my search for the Lyndheart. A quest that could ensure the safety or destruction of the entire human race. I thought your presence, your uniqueness, held meaning, a key, to my search. Yet now I wonder, perhaps you are a distraction. To slow me down entirely."

96

That stung. For some reason, I cared what Edrick thought of me. And I assumed we were becoming friends, of some weird sort or another. Maybe he didn't need to lie to me at all. Maybe the lie was how I felt for him, or how I thought he felt about me.

Maybe I *was* just some obligation.

"I'm sorry," I said. "I'm tired. And I—"

I found myself halfway across the small shack, looking down at him. I could see Edrick enough to tell he was miserable. Despite everything he was, had been through, could do, he was still just a man. A man trying to protect some silly girl who made things difficult for him despite his best efforts to keep her safe. Just a cold, lonely human. Unsure. Feeling lost.

Like myself.

"I'm sorry."

"Please stop apologizing."

"Well, then, thank you." I yawned. "For… everything."

"You are welcome, Brianna."

Morning came too quickly. I was too cold and hungry to stay asleep. And my dreams had haunted me more than anything else. When I finally opened my tired, gritty eyes, I saw Edrick standing at the entrance, looking out into the sunrise. Had he stayed awake all night? I began to wonder if he slept at all. Maybe after hundreds of years, he discovered some secret to not need sleep?

I sat up, rubbing the sand from my eyes. I still felt tired, but less so than I had before. How long had I even been asleep? The night before seemed disorienting. Without the moon or stars, without a watch, who knew when I had begun wandering around, when Laura-Lei and then Edrick found me? Who knew what time I had finally fallen asleep? All I could tell was that I felt better but not completely rested, and that it was still early in the morning as the sun barely drifted above the horizon.

"Hi?" I asked. I knew Edrick would have heard me stirring. Yet he hadn't turned to look or even said anything.

"I need to check something out." His voice sounded flat, tired. "I need to get back on track towards finding the Lyndheart before Dragon does. There is bottled water and some food in a bag in the corner." Turning, I found myself barely able to look at him. His haggard face seemed to have aged overnight, losing the warmth and friendliness he once wore. Blue-gray eyes now seemed gloomier and harder, like the unyielding face of a mountain. One hand rested firmly on the end of his sheathed sword. He was no longer dressed in the jeans and sweater that once belonged to Mark. For some reason, I felt a pang of sadness about that. While I was more used to seeing him in his armor than street clothes, I had begun to look at him differently when not dressed like a warrior. I could tell he had patched up the leather armor at some point. I don't know how he wasn't freezing in it. I still had the large felt coat wrapped around me and *I* was cold.

"Edrick—"

"I realized last night that you need to make a decision," he spoke slowly, as if he were lecturing me. "You do not want to be a Summoner. Laura-Lei said she has removed Dragon's tracking spell from you. If you choose to take the risk, then go and find your normal life. Go find Mark. I promise I will not follow you this time. You know the risks of coming with me, of what I will require from you. You will need to leave everything behind. Be studious in your training. Above all, I will require that you listen to me and follow my directions. I did not give you much choice before." I couldn't bear to look at him as he paused. "Think it over today. That should be long enough."

I still couldn't look as I heard him step out into the dawn, his leather boots crunching on old, frozen leaves. My chest once again felt as if it were being squeezed with a belt of nails. It seemed strange to think of what just happened this way, and yet... it felt like I had been dumped. As if I had cheated on Mark with some other guy, and now that guy had broken up with me.

Somewhat choked up and knowing I should not have felt that way, I scooted over to the bag Edrick had left. I shoved a bottle of water into one of the oversized pockets, opening a second and downing it. I coughed a little. How long had it been since I'd had anything to drink? A day and a half? One day? It seemed so much longer.

The bag also held an assortment of snacks. I shoved a small bag of trail mix and a granola bar into the opposite pocket when my hand brushed something. I pulled it out. A price tag for the coat. Holding it in my hand, I remembered Edrick saying he never carried money with him but convinced people that he needed things from them. Basically, I clarified to myself, he stole them. Stole the coat. The food and water. I couldn't think about that now. Tearing off the tag, I dropped it to the ground and hurriedly ripped open a second granola bar for my breakfast.

Halfway through, my eyes drifted to the corner I had slept in. And leaning against the wall stood my staff. I paused mid-bite, staring at it like an alien. Foreign, yet so familiar.

My hand could feel the worn smoothness of the wood, the weight of it, oddly balanced. My eyes stared at the shard tied towards the top with a single word etched across it in an ancient language – Ascalon. The faint tinkling of metal, wood, and glass resonated in my ears still.

I stepped back, standing in the same doorway Edrick had left maybe thirty minutes before. Standing there, I recalled the pain I had been through. The injuries, anxiety attacks. I thought of all the experiences I had been through. So much in such a short period of time.

It hit me, everything I had now lost. Simple things like my car and job. Personal belongings. More important things like a relationship, connections with others.

The loss of life. The strangers who had died at the hospital.

Kara.

Edrick was giving me an out. A chance to reclaim that life.

I knew what I wanted.

Stepping out of the shack, I picked a direction, south, and began to walk.

I found myself on the other side of town, several miles from the hospital. You could call it the backroads section between towns. I thought of hitching a ride, but maybe one car passed me by during all that time.

I knew roughly where I was now that I had found my way to a road. Had I been driving I could have made it home in twenty minutes. But walking, it took a few hours. Alone with my thoughts, I thought about what Edrick had said. I was free from Dragon's tracker. For the first time in a long time, I was doing something normal. Non-threatening.

Time flew by despite the chill in the air. Before I knew it, I had happened across my road. For the first time in a long time, my heart began to beat in excitement, not fear. I knew the house I rented was going to be a mess. And somehow, I would need to contact my landlord and explain to her why the bedroom window had exploded inward and needed replacing. Then, I remembered, rent had to be due any day now. Maybe I could ask my parents for a loan until I could figure out my car situation, get a new job.

As I rounded the bend in the road, I realized, my heart sinking, that I had underestimated my situation.

I knew I hadn't been home in a few days. Yet it seemed hard to believe that so much had changed in that time. The small, ranch house I rented had basically been leveled. Even from this distance, I could still smell the acrid taint of burn. Faint, wispy tendrils still wafted above what used to be my home. My clothes. My laptop.

My life.

Tears began falling before I even realized I had started crying.

How did this happen? How much more was I going to lose?

Between this and the hospital incident, my parents and sister must have been notified. I had missed Thanksgiving with no visit. No call. They would have heard about Kara's death from friend's in town. The deaths at the hospital. My being taken hostage surely must have been on the news. Someone would have notified them of my home burning down. What would they think? Was it possible they were even on their way up to find me, help me?

What would Mark think?

I heard a car turning down the road. Something in me made me panic. Brushing tears from my eyes, I stepped off the road and crouched down behind the tree line.

A county sheriffs' car, white with red lettering and bold insignias, drove down, clearly going under the speed limit. As it passed, I watched a man looking around both sides of the road.

I stayed hidden behind the tree line, crouched in the scrubs, until the car was out of sight. Why hadn't I flagged him down? Why hadn't I asked for help?

Edrick's warning stuck to me like a permanent stain. To watch out. To trust no one. Dragon's magic tracer might have been removed by Laura-Lei, but that didn't mean he would stop looking for me. Maybe, he would be looking even harder. And what did the Shadow Man want? What was his method of finding me? Edrick had mentioned that the hospital incident had been all over the news, in the mouths of all the locals on the street.

Everyone would know me by now. Everyone would be looking for me.

Was that the intention? Could I trust anyone? Why would I question my safety around law enforcement? Unless someone worked for either Dragon or the Shadow Man, and how could I tell who they were, and what they wanted.

I literally could trust no one.

I felt sick, stepping back on the road. Was I really still in this much danger? I thought Edrick had been exaggerating. But the more I thought about it, the more I saw the signs — the burnt house, cops driving by, looking for something, or someone — I couldn't avoid the truth.

Mark. I had to find Mark. As much as I didn't exactly want to stay his girlfriend, I could trust him at least. His would be a place to stay. He really did care a lot about me, was always concerned about me. I began to believe he was the only one who could accept me and protect me until I could figure out what the hell was going on. What I would need to do to return to normal.

Relatively speaking, Mark's house wasn't that far away. About a five-minute car ride. Yet again, stuck walking, it took significantly longer to walk. Especially when paranoia made me hop off the side of the road, hiding in ditches and behind trees and brush every time I heard a car approaching.

Early afternoon arrived before I found myself in front of Mark's house. Beneath the open coat and light sweater, I sweated. I had finished the bottle of water and the rest of the snacks in my pocket as I had turned onto the road. More than anything, I wanted to climb into his shower, pop something quick into the microwave, and take a long nap. My chest and head hurt from the anxiety I felt at every car's passing. My legs burned from walking so much.

Drawing on a ridiculously small reserve of energy, I nearly jogged the last quarter mile to his house. His was a small, two-story home he owned. It sat off the road, neighbors visible to either side, but far enough away that you felt you had some privacy. Turning into his driveway, I dashed to the door, beating it hard with my fist. I turned, keeping my eyes and ears open for the sound of any approaching vehicles.

101

After a minute, I turned back to the door, panicking. I rapped on the door once again, pausing to jingle the handle in case it was unlocked.

He had to be home!

I tried to think what day of the week it was. Maybe he had to go into work. Was it a weekday or the weekend? *Shit,* I realized with a start. I didn't even know if it was still November! I knocked on the door one more time, to no response. Mark didn't have a garage, and I didn't see his truck in the driveway, something I hadn't noticed till now.

Trying not to cry, I sat down on the step. My heart was racing, and my chest was burning something fierce, like I couldn't breathe. I had to stay calm. Think this through.

What do I do now? Maybe I could wait here until he gets back home. Maybe he just went to the store.

But he would have heard what happened to me and the house. Was he out looking for me? If he was, how long would he be gone, how long would I have to wait?

If he did come home and find me here, would he actually protect me, or would he bring me to the authorities? And if he did that… could I say no?

What if he said no?

"What are you doing here?"

The voice startled me. I swore and jumped to my feet. "Mark, fuck, I—"

The look on Edrick's face made my chest hurt even more.

"Edrick? But how—"

The look of confusion and panic on his face made me stop.

"Brianna? What are you doing at this place?"

"Me? This is Mark's house. I… I came to talk to him."

As soon as I said his name, I saw Edrick's face change. "So, you have made a decision."

"Edrick, I… I can't be a Summoner. I just… I don't have it in me." I shook my head. "But what are you doing here? At Mark's house?"

"I am following a lead on the Lyndheart." He ran a hand over his face, gripping the base of his sword tight with one hand. "If you have decided, Brianna, then this no longer concerns you. Step aside."

An uneasiness began to stir in my gut. Why would some lead bring him here? "Edrick, Mark may be annoying at times, but he's not a monster."

"This no longer concerns you."

"If it involves Mark it does!"

"You are no longer a Summoner."

"So, everything I went through, everything I now have to fix in my life, none of that matters anymore? I'm supposed to just leave all that behind?"

Edrick sighed, looking down at me. "I did not choose that path for you. You did. I offered you the choice to protect yourself and others. Continuously, you walked away. Choosing to return to the past does not change anything, that is not how the world works. You are burying your head in the sand and will only continue to hurt yourself and others. I have tried to help you, Brianna. Yet until you own the decision for yourself, nothing is going to change." He took a step closer, towering over me. This close, I could smell his spiced breath. The oil on his leather armor. I knew what he was, what he could do. I felt intimidated. Called out.

"How many times will you give up because it is hard? Not realizing that either choice comes with dangers. If you choose to hide in the sand, then this is—"

"Oh, really?" I scoffed. I tried to take a step closer, planting my fists on my hips. I wanted to punch him so bad. Was he really so dense? Did he really think it was all so easy? Oh, sure, become a weirdo Summoner and lose your entire life and step into a world trying to kill you at every turn. Or forget it all and go back to your normal life but be defenseless and hunted and killed by two beings who didn't even know you because you were something you didn't even understand? "It's that simple, huh? Did you remember what happened to me? Did you see what happened to everything I once owned? What happened to everyone who has been around me when these monsters attack? And you think I'm just burying my head in the sand?" I felt my face flush with anger. "Maybe you need to get yours out of your Guardian ass and take a second to realize what my life has suddenly been turned into!"

"You want to be normal, lead an ordinary, dull, human life." Edrick snarled. His face shone no compassion. "And I told you, it can never be the same. You can pretend what happened never did. You can hope that Dragon, the Shadow Man, Laura-Lei, will never find you again. Yet deep down, you know they will."

Tears blurred my eyes as my chest once again felt as if it had been crushed. "I just want to live, damnit! I don't want to be responsible for any more deaths. Monsters. Humans. I don't want to be hurt anymore. Why is that so hard to ask for?"

"That is life," he said without emotion. "Life. Death. Most never get to choose what to do with one or the other. You have the choice of both. And no, it cannot be easy. Should not be. Life and death… they are more precious than any one thing." His eyes stared hard at me, and I had to turn away. "More than any one person. There is no going back. Ever. If you choose to try and pretend to be mundane, then you risk your life and those of everyone else who becomes part of your life. I have the lives and futures of others to think about. More so than that of one girl."

"Just… go away, Edrick, before Mark shows up."

"No."

"Look, this is my decision and my boyfriend's house." It felt weird saying it. Especially in front of him. I brushed at my eyes, still mad, yet I quickly began to lose my nerve. "You need to go before he gets back."

"Have you spoken to him already then? I need to search inside." Using his shoulder, Edrick pushed me away from the door, grabbing the handle with his other hand.

"Hey!" I shouted, stumbling off the concrete pad. "You can't just do that!"

"Brianna, I—"

We both whipped our heads towards the road as a dog began barking. The husky pulled at the end of a leash, held back, barely, by an older woman in her forties or fifties.

"Sorry!" The woman shouted from the edge of the road. "Kodi doesn't like fighting! Miss, are you okay?" She eyed Edrick suspiciously.

"No!" I shouted back. "This man is trying to break into my boyfriend's house!"

The woman had one hand halfway out of her pocket, holding a cellphone. Behind me, I could hear Edrick rattling the doorknob. "Hey, aren't you that girl they're looking for? Yeah, and your—" She gasped. "You're the man who kidnapped her, aren't you?"

My heart skipped a beat. I opened my mouth to protest.

The dog suddenly stopped pulling, instead peeling its muzzle back in a vicious snarl. Its attention turned from us to the closest house next to Mark's. An old farmhouse with a vine covered partially dilapidated barn. The fur raised all along the back of the dog's neck. Its eyes widened to show mainly whites as it began to pull wildly the way it had come. The woman scolded it as she dropped her phone, trying and failing to gain control over the dog.

That's when I felt it. I reached out and grabbed Edrick's arm. Already I could feel something powerful splitting my mind. Hunger, anticipation. I was so close. Yet I could also sense my own fear, confusion. "No," I mumbled under my breath. "Something's here."

I could hear and see out of the corner of my eyes as Edrick pulled out his sword.

"Run!" I screamed at the woman.

The barn doors exploded outward. Rotting shards of wood sprayed in all directions as a large mass of fur flew from the dark opening. In mere seconds, it raced the short distance across the yards. The beast had a lumbering gait, its back sloped, with a stubby tail, short, stocky back legs, and long, reaching front legs. Golden-tan colored fur like sand and spotted with dark brown and black markings stood out thick and in places matted.

I would have said a hyena had escaped the zoo, except this thing stood significantly taller and had two heads. Two! Except... I had to squint. The two heads almost appeared to be as one for a moment, and then a single head the next, and yet again, they were apart from each other. One was the head of a massive hyena, the other, of what appeared to be human, yet it seemed to be constantly shifting.

I didn't mean to feel it, yet it came to me all the same. The beast had dueling minds. One kept shifting; kept becoming one, then separating again. With my own thoughts and feelings, it became confusing and disorienting.

My hand fell from Edrick's arm as he stepped in front of me, mostly blocking me. I could feel more than see the monster approach the woman. The husky snarled and snapped more violently now, thrashing at the end of the leash to get away. As if bored, the woman stood up and dropped the leash. She didn't turn toward her dog. She didn't seem to realize at all what she had done, instead growing fixated on the beast. Not in fear though. Stoic, as if hypnotized.

I called out to her again, but I couldn't seem to make out what I said. I heard another in my head. A deep, rich, melodic man's voice. I couldn't hear the words, but the powerful, alluring sound pulled at me all the same.

Edrick looked at me saying something. I didn't understand the words as a snarl filled my mind. He grabbed my shoulder too tight in one hand, shaking me so hard I thought I might get whiplash. "Brianna! Snap out of it! Do not listen to it! Do not listen to it," he repeated.

"Huh?" I blinked. I could still hear the man's voice, but I could hear Edrick's better now.

Edrick stopped shaking me, but still held my shoulder tight. "Please tell me you brought the staff," he whispered, his eyes glancing up at the beast. In the few seconds that transpired, his face had gone white.

"No, I—"

The hyena beast crept up to the woman, who stood trembling and smiling.

Larger than any I had ever seen at the zoo or on TV, it stood in front of the woman, its head towering over hers. The man part of its head shifted, still speaking to her. Though the edges were blurred, the man appeared dark, handsome, sparkling black eyes engaging and locked onto hers. The hyena one, on the back of the man's head, when it was visible, would roll its golden eyes as if searching for something.

"We have to get you out of here," Edrick grabbed my arm with one hand. "It is here for you."

"What's it going to do to that woman?" I asked, trembling. I wanted to shout, but I found I could barely whisper in fear. "Edrick, we have to—"

"I cannot do anything," he snarled. He yanked hard on my arm, and I cried out. "We cannot do anything. If you had brought your staff..." Shaking his head, he began to drag me towards the back of Mark's house and the woods behind it.

In my mind I could hear the hyena head snarling and yipping. The man's head, though, felt calm. I turned my head, trying to see what was going on. The beast now leaned over the woman so close, he could have kissed her. I stumbled, not breaking my stare as Edrick continued to drag me. "Please, we have to do something!"

"Look away," he said, grunting as he tried to pull me harder around the corner of the house. "Brianna, do not look!"

I jerked my arm and while it didn't break his hold, I was able to look around the corner of the house. And quickly wished I hadn't.

The man did lean in, the woman ecstatic. She looked like someone who had a religious awakening. From here, I could make out her flushed face and rapidly moving lips. The whites of her eyes shown, unblinking. She began lifting her hands. Yet before she could touch the beast, the heads shifted. The man's face phased away for a second. The hyena face inverted itself, now facing the woman. Its mouth gaped horribly wide, filled with massive, sharp canines, and thick molars in the back. The golden eyes roved wildly. I could feel its hunger, its trembling excitement. In the same instant, the man's head appeared in the back of the hyena's head. Its mouth stretched open as if crying out, tears streaming from his brown eyes. Like the hyena, they rolled around until they spotted me. I felt a tug in my head, a need to be drawn closer, a hunger so deep, I can't describe it.

Even from here, I could hear the snarl of the hyena. Yet I was spared what happened next. Edrick grabbed me around the waist and violently threw me over his shoulder. He began to run. I didn't try fighting it. I started crying. Even though I couldn't see it, I knew what was happening. I could feel it in my mind. I could feel the soft flesh, the crunch of bone. The satisfaction of it feeding a hunger it had known for a long time as a rich, warm wetness dripped from its face.

Deep down, I could feel the man's mind. He knew who the real prey was. So, did I.

"It's after me. It's after me!"

Edrick ran. And ran. He began to breathe heavily. Finally, rasping for air, he dropped me down to the ground unceremoniously. He bent over a moment, taking in massive gulps of air. Despite the cold, sweat rolled down his face, a cloud of warm condensed air forming a halo around his head. Rocking and hugging my knees, I sobbed. "That could have been me. That should have been me. It was waiting. It was waiting for me!"

"Get up," he wheezed, straightening up some. His breathing had slowed enough so he could talk.

"It was after me. It ate her, but the other half—"

"Kishi," he snapped. "Half hyena, half man. It lures you in, steals your will with its charm. When you are close enough, you cannot resist them. No one can. Not even a Guardian." He lifted his head, looking at me, terror in his eyes. "I have never actually seen one. But its presence here confirms my fear. I do not know if it would have eaten you, Brianna. Or whether Dragon or the Shadow Man sent it. All I know for certain is that even though the tracker is gone from you, they still know where you are, and are throwing everything they can to get to you."

"But I—"

Edrick shook his head firmly, standing straight. "What are you not understanding? Sometimes we do not have the luxury of pursuing what we want!"

Startled, I wiped my nose with the coat sleeve. He had never shouted at me like this before. "Wasn't there anything you could have done?"

He stared hard at me. "No. But *we* could have."

I felt like I was going to be sick. "If I had the staff with me."

"If you had managed to summon something, anything, to distract it, I would have had a chance. I would have tried," he replied quietly. "It would have taken at least another Guardian, or I suspect, even a semi-skilled Summoner. Alone? It would have used its charm and then killed me and then gotten to you."

Bile rolled up into the back of my throat. "Then, she died, because of me. Because it was looking for me. Because I didn't do anything. Because…"

"Yes," Edrick admitted, though I could tell it hurt him to say it. His face looked pinched, and he quickly looked away. "She died, another person died, because you were too concerned about how you wanted to live your life, and not how your life is affecting others."

My head was spinning. I felt like passing out. Me. It was all because of me. The pain that gripped my chest made it almost difficult to breathe. I wanted to walk away from all of this. I thought it would make everything better, easier. Yet the monster still found me. If Edrick hadn't been there, I would likely have died as well.

"Let us at least make good of her sacrifice," he mumbled, grabbing my wrist tightly. "We need to get back to the staff. Eventually, the kishi will finish and come searching for you. The wards I put up around the shed should protect us for some time. It is best that we are hidden and have the staff on hand."

We stuck to the fields, yards, and woods on the way back. I was utterly lost, but Edrick somehow knew the way as if it were his home. By the time we reached it, the sky had fallen into darkness, and a cold wind had risen. I felt so raw and numb at the same time. Plopping down onto the icy log, I didn't feel as if I were alive, but a shadow in someone else's dream. Nightmare.

The shed hardly blocked any of the freezing wind. My stomach hurt. Hell, everything hurt. Even my soul. Thankfully, the coat was oversized. I did my best to curl up inside of it, folding the arms across my chest, drawing my knees and some of my legs inside under the waist band. With the hoodie enclosing almost my whole head, I finally felt as if I could be warm. Alone.

Edrick sat near the entrance. In the near total darkness, I could still see the glint of his eyes occasionally looking my way, alternating out into the woods. His sword sat across his lap, ready at a moment's notice. Despite the lack of light, I could tell he was exhausted, at the end of his rope. When was the last time he had eaten, slept? His mood the past two days had changed. Darker, shorter of temper. Fear had become a new expression for him, and that frightened me. Every choice I made, I realized, drained him more. Even when I had chosen to walk away from it all, when he had gone off to follow his lead, I still managed to pop up like a bad penny and mess everything up.

I think I fell asleep for a few minutes, maybe an hour. I had no way to tell in the midst of an early winter night, in a shack, in the middle of an overgrown and forgotten apple orchard. When I woke up, Edrick still remained in the same spot. I wondered for a moment if he had finally fallen asleep. Then I saw him turn his head a bit. He looked miserable, depleted.

"Why were you at Mark's?"

Slowly, his eyes met mine. "I told you. I followed a lead there. A beast who might have known where the Lyndheart was." His gaze turned back toward the orchard. "Though I doubt the kishi would have known. Why were you there?"

I shivered under the coat. "I hoped maybe Mark could help me out."

"I am sorry, Brianna. But if the kishi remained when Mark arrived home, he will be dead."

That possibility hadn't even crossed my mind all afternoon. I assumed the kishi would have hunted us after eating the woman. But what if it stayed, somehow knowing my relationship with Mark? *Two more, dead. Because of me.*

Still cold, I uncurled myself and moved beside him, unzipping the coat. He watched in confused silence as I plopped down on the makeshift bench beside him. Pulling one arm out of the sleeve, I draped half the coat over his shoulder and most of his back. It wasn't much, but the coat was warm, warmer than his leathers.

"What are you doing?" he asked.

"What do you think?"

"You should rest."

"Yeah, you too. Just, shut up and enjoy the heat."

It felt strange, sitting so close to him. Our hips and shoulders touched. I could feel his body begin to relax, the warmth from my body and the coat thawing him out. As if starving for heat, I felt him lean into me. I could smell his spiced breath. Already it was becoming soothing, familiar. I remembered him telling me — what, a week, two weeks ago now? — that he had a quest that brought him over here to the U.S. Instead, he had spent all this time with me, doing what? Protecting me. Supporting me. Trying to train me. And all I had done was…

Get in the way. Be a brat. Ruin his cover, I finally admitted to myself. And as a result…

I shuddered, remembering the feeling in my mind, which was probably worse than if I had seen it happen.

How many people now? What would have happened if I believed him from the beginning? If I had trained from the beginning to be a Summoner? Would they have all lived?

"I'm sorry," I murmured.

"Do not be, Brianna."

Edrick moved, startling me from my weary thoughts. Reaching out with his left arm, he wrapped it around my shoulder, under the coat. I wasn't sure what to think. Was he worried I was cold? Trying to show me I could relax, sleep? He gave my upper arm a squeeze, and it felt as if he were holding me tighter. Was he worried I was going to leave? He had sounded so mad though, why would he keep trying to protect me, put up with me? Especially when the last thing I wanted to do was train to be a Summoner.

A myriad of jumbled thoughts bombarded my mind. I had way more questions, and no answers for any of them. I wanted to think. I knew I needed to decide. Knowing things could never, ever go back the way they were before, what was I willing to do to force them to be that way? Instead, I felt so comforted, so at peace, I closed my eyes, and didn't realize till morning, I had fallen asleep.

CHAPTER 12

Dreams consumed my sleep. People dying. Me consistently failing to summon anything helpful. And finally, the worst scenario, I had summoned that giant thing with the three heads and wings. Ascalon. And I watch, unable to move, unable to do anything, as Edrick looked at me with terror and defeat in his eyes. He approached the Chaos creature with faint determination. And then I watched as he failed. Instead, it tore him apart as he screamed and cursed my name while I stood paralyzed, feeling every single head revel in its meal.

Despite the freezing cold morning, I woke up in a sweat, which cooled way too fast and left me chilled and shivering. Edrick had gone. I wasn't sure what to do. Should I stay and wait for him? All I knew was I was famished beyond belief. Headache and dizziness gnawed at my mind. Dull, cramping pains in my gut made me want to double over.

The coat had slipped off. I must have fallen asleep, and Edrick laid me down at the foot of the log we sat on. I remembered the night before, and a warmth spread up my neck into my cheeks. I was scared. I knew, deep down, I was falling for him. Had been. As much as I didn't want to admit it, as much as I kept saying Mark was still my boyfriend... I never had anyone care about me and sacrifice so much for me as Edrick did, despite my efforts otherwise. Would Mark ever have stood between me and a host of monsters? Would he have ever fought them off with nothing more than a sword, all just to protect me? It was such an archaic notion, especially in this day and age. And yet... those acts spoke more in volume than words of affection or gifts.

But the thought, no matter how small, was impossible. We were from two different worlds. Cultures. Hell, if Edrick was telling the truth, we were centuries apart. I didn't think I could ever understand or accept his world. I felt mental from just the past couple of weeks. I couldn't imagine living, barely surviving, months or years of this.

And it would never be a real relationship. Not like we could go out on a dinner date. Hang out at places like ordinary people. I would be a Summoner, and he was a Guardian. That didn't sound like the kind of lives conducive to relationships.

It was a silly, stupid, thought, yet my brain couldn't seem to let go of it.

My presence, too, was obviously keeping him from his real quest. And his presence kept me from the life I wanted to live. I needed to get him far away from me. His quest was here. After yesterday's events, it was clear I couldn't stay here. If I could get access to a car, then I could possibly drive to my family's home in Pennsylvania. I have no idea what I would do after that. But I needed to do something. I needed to get away from everything.

I had to get away from Edrick.

For his sake and mine.

But how?

That's when I remembered I had a fairly close friend in high school who lived not too far from where we were. Assuming she remembered me, and wasn't freaked out by the media hype, maybe she would be willing to help me out.

Edrick returned within a few minutes of my waking. He had donned the sweater and jeans over his leathers once again. Although he looked a little less exhausted than he had the night before, I could see on his face the strain he was under.

"Hey, um," I broke the silence. It sounded strange in the stillness. But I didn't want to chicken out. This was too important. "I think a high school friend of mine still lives around here. We were good friends, and just kinda, you know, lost track staying in touch with each other. I'm thinking of asking her for help. Maybe she will lend us her car."

Edrick looked at me strangely. "Why do we need a car?"

I gestured around the shack. "We can't stay here like this. I mean, we don't have any food or water with us. It's going to be snowing soon—"

"Where would you go?"

"I dunno. Do you even have a plan at this point?" I asked. "We can't just stay here in the woods all winter. What are you even accomplishing?"

112

Edrick sat, scowling. "We cannot form anything until we know why Dragon and Shadow Man want you."

"At least let me go ask my friend if she will help us, maybe borrow her car. Let's get away from here, somewhere safer, where we can at least figure out what to do next."

Exhaling, Edrick nodded. "Fine."

"I'll take the staff with me," I replied, climbing to my feet. "I'll only use it if I have to."

"I am coming with you," he said, standing. "I will stay out of sight, but I do not dare leave you alone, especially not after the kishi attack."

I felt a chill go down my spine, though it seemed all too familiar now. Was this my new reality, where gruesome, violent acts would become the norm?

We walked in silence out of the woods and to the main road. I tried to remember, from here, which direction to go to Amy's house. No more than two miles away, I figured, hoping she still lived with her parents. Her family had never been well off, and Amy never wanted much out of life, especially in the way of material things. It started coming back to me as we walked through the dusting of snow, close enough to the road so I could remember where we were going, but at Edrick's suggestion, deep enough in the trees that no one would see us.

When I spotted the house, I realized how stupid close we lived to each other. We used to be so close in school, yet we had fallen out of touch over the years. *Maybe after this,* I thought to myself. There were going to be a lot of changes in my life after all of this. Maybe one of them would be reconnecting with Amy.

I had Edrick stay across the road behind the tree line. From the road, he blended in, just another shadow in the woods, broken up by the branches and defiant weeds, now long dead.

Two cars sat in the driveway, one which I knew was her parents. An old, beat-up 1980's Volkswagen they swore would continue running long after they died. I didn't recognize the other, though it looked hardly any newer than her folks. It looked like some kind of Honda from the 90's, held together in more than a few places with duct tape. I assumed it was Amy's. At the front door, I knocked, waiting while I heard a small dog barking wildly. I could hear someone scolding the pup as they unlocked and opened the door.

Amy hadn't changed much. She had cut her brown hair shorter, up to her chin. Her soft brown eyes still held the sweet innocence they always did, still too big for her narrow but kind face. A huge smile spread, replacing the look of absolute shock as she stepped out onto the landing with wide arms. "Oh my god, Brianna!"

I couldn't help but smile as I stepped into the house to get out of the cold, hugging her back though not quite as tight as she held me. "Hi Amy! How's it going?"

"You look like shit, girl," she chided, holding me away from her and gawking. "I'd ask how you've been, but…" She blew a raspberry. "You've been all over the news. Hurry and get your ass in here!" As she grabbed my hand, she pinched her nose with the other. "Oh, my god, you reek. Now I know why all the officials want you, that smell has got to be illegal!"

I couldn't help but laugh as she pulled me inside, looking around the yard before shutting the door. Amy had always been really sweet and brutally honest. What would have been a criticism from anyone else was always raw love and concern from her. "Yeah, it's been a rough few weeks."

"Yeah, so I hear." She began, drawing me deeper into the house. "I… I heard what happened to Kara. You two were still friends, right? I'm so sorry."

I cringed as I told her, vaguely, that yes, I heard she had passed. I didn't get into the how or why, thinking it would be better to act as if I had simply heard about it happening instead of being there. Amy did gloss over the fact that a lot of weird things had been on the news lately and how people either thought it was government conspiracies, or the end of the world.

"Hey, so, you know you have been all over the news, right?"

We were in her bedroom. She had shoved a large, reheated cup of coffee into my hands while she went through her closet, pulling out a towel and some clothes for me. "Um, I haven't really seen the news or anything. But someone mentioned I was."

"Okay, so like, what the fuck is going on? Is any of it true?"

I felt my heart flutter fearfully as my stomach turned. "What are they saying?"

"That you were kidnapped from the hospital by some stranger with a sword. They said you were in imminent danger and that the man was armed and dangerous. Then, depending on who you ask, either the same man burnt down your house, or that it was gang related."

"Ed—I mean, he wasn't dangerous," I started slowly, realizing I needed to be careful. She was my friend and all. I really doubt she even knew anything about the beasts or Dragon or the Shadow Man. Yet after everything I had been through, I was feeling a bit paranoid. "The guy said something was after me and that he was trying to help me. He might have been a little crazy, but I dunno. He kept me safe, at least he believed he did."

"He didn't hurt you in any way?"

"No!" I blurted.

"So why do you look like you've been through hell and back?" She eyed me suspiciously, taking the mug and shoving the towel and clothes into my arms.

"Something happened to my house and I got scared. I didn't have a car or money, and my boyfriend, Mark, was out of town, so I've been... camping, in the woods."

"Did you know your family is coming up from Pennsylvania to look for you?"

It felt like my heart stopped. I couldn't tell if I was excited or terrified. "How-how do you know?"

"They found my old number and gave me a call and asked if I knew what the hell was going on, if I had seen you at all. They have been asking everyone they can think of in town. They have everyone looking for you." She glanced around her room, lowering her voice as she leaned in. "I bet the government has people looking for you, too, after all the weird shit people have been saying has been going on. Is it true?"

I swallowed, trying not to panic. All I wanted to do was to see my parents, to see Elizabeth. Somehow, I knew if they came here, they would be in danger. It seemed safer for them to wait for me to come to them. "Amy. Can you call them back and tell them to wait for me? It's not safe for them to come here."

"So, the weird things... they're true?" Her eyes grew wide. "Should, like, I be leaving town?"

"No, I... I dunno. I just know they can't be here. Can you tell them I'll come to them?"

Amy nibbled on her lower lip nervously. "Yeah, I'll pull their number from the caller ID. So, what exactly should I tell them? You are going down to them then? But, what about the creatures' people are talking about? Won't—"

I held up a hand, shaking my head. "Amy, please. Just, just tell them to wait for me."

Amy looked at me skeptically. "Fine, fine. You know, I'm not going to pry, that ain't me, but shit. At least let me help you out, okay? And when or if you want to tell me what's really going on—"

I wrapped an arm around her and hugged tightly. I could have cried. Still the same, supporting Amy. Now I felt really bad waiting so long to reach out to her.

The shower was the best in my life. I could have stood under the hot water for hours. Dirt, sweat, and grime sluiced off. I hadn't realized my hair had gotten so tangled, and it took ten minutes just to comb it out. The warm water soothed my tired eyes and sinuses, easing all the aches in my muscles.

"I called your folks house. Got a hold of Elizabeth and she said she would tell your parents," Amy shouted from outside of the bathroom, interrupting my vacation from reality. "Can I help you out with anything else?"

I winced, worried I was about to overstep her offer. "I, ah, could really borrow a car so I can get down to my parent's house in PA. Mine was destroyed, and I don't have a way to rent one."

"Oh, sure, no problem," she replied. "I inherited my parent's winter beater before they moved. I'll loan you that one and take mine to work."

"The old Volkswagen?"

"Trust me," I heard her laugh, "my car definitely won't make it to Pennsylvania."

I let out a sigh of relief, then started laughing, not realizing how much I had worked myself up about it. "Thank you so much, Amy. You don't know how much that means to me! So, where are you working?"

"Know that old motel by the highway? My folks bought it, and I run it while they travel across country."

"Um, isn't that…" I began, trying to recall the motel. The only one I knew of was run down and rather scummy. The kind of place usually used by people more by the hour than by the night.

"Haha, yeah, you know the one," she chuckled before I could finish. "It's good money though, for basically little work. I'm essentially my own boss. Lots of time to read my books and watch my shows while running the desk."

The idea hit me. It was perfect and would solve all my issues. At least, in the short term. "Amy, I hate to ask," I said before I had even finished the plan that was going through my mind, "but I have a friend that kind of needs a place like that to stay for a day or two. Until he figures out where he has to go next—"

"Mystery guy needs a place to chill before leaving town," she interrupted, saving me. "Yeah, I can help you out, as long as you promise he won't burn the place down or go kidnapping anyone."

"He's not like that," I admitted, still not ready to tell her everything. "I went with him. I wasn't kidnapped. I-I'll explain someday."

After getting cleaned up and dressed in fresh jeans and a three-quarter sleeve sweater that felt warm and wonderful instead of thin and cold, she fed me a hot lunch and more coffee. She handed me two sets of keys, one for the car, and another looked like an old room key, as I was finishing up. "The car only has about half a tank in it," she said, pressing some money into my hands. "And here's the room key. It's the cleanest. I try to keep one... well, you know, in case I have to stay the night."

I hugged Amy one more time. "Thank you so much. You have no idea what this means to me."

Amy laughed again. "Just call me once you are at your folks and are safe, okay? Don't worry about the car. We'll figure it out."

I stepped out of the house, feeling refreshed and alive. I felt... normal. Which only nailed home what I had to do next. Snow started falling as I got into the car. Pulling out of the driveway, I saw Edrick peeking through the tree line. I pointed to the right as I pulled out onto the road. Half a mile, away from any houses that could see, I pulled over. Edrick caught up, carrying the staff. "That took quite a while," he said. His eyes looked me up and down. "Do you think it was wise to take the time to refresh yourself here?"

"She wouldn't let me leave until I cleaned up and ate," I replied. "Amy's a good friend. I feel bad for not catching up with her until now."

"Are you hurt?"

"Huh?"

He nodded to me. "Your eyes. You look as if you are in pain."

I glanced up at the rearview mirror. I did look horrible. Clean, but miserable. My pale face only accentuated my wide and tired, teary eyes. Inside, I felt my heart racing, chest tightening.

"Look, just get in the car."

Opening the door, he slid into the passenger seat, shifting his sword so it lay more across his lap while he set the staff so it sat between us, extending into the back seat.

"And buckle."

He did this, too, with no resistance.

I put the car into drive and took a deep breath. "I made a decision. I can't do this anymore," I finally blurted. I wanted to say it differently. Carefully scripted lines between Amy's and here seemed to fly off on me. It didn't come out the way I wanted it to, but it came out. "I can't be doing this anymore. I mean, I guess I will take my chances. Someone, somewhere, will be able to protect me, right? I am going to look, find someone on my own, who can do that."

I could feel his tension without even looking at him. "No. No one can protect you. A Guardian might, for a while. But even then, it would be expected that you learn to defend yourself. There is too much at stake elsewhere in the world for… anyone else to attach himself to you for life. And there are many Guardians who may want to kill you to protect the planet from you consistently tearing open the realms."

Tears started streaming from my eyes. "I just… I've been thinking, the past several days, and I just, I just don't want the kind of life—"

"Yes, you have said it before. You would rather have a short life than that of a Summoner."

I shook my head. "No, I don't want either." I sniffled. "I don't want to die. I… just want my life. I just want it to be my choice."

"Even if others die?"

I didn't bother answering. He knew the answer. I knew the answer. Yet I knew, deep down, there *had* to be another way! There had to be a way, someone maybe, who would know how to allow me to live without endangering others!

He stewed for a moment. "Where are you taking me, then?"

I bit my lip. "To a motel. Don't worry, an old friend works there, and, well, they are used to all sorts of types coming and going. She won't ask questions, and she won't say anything to anyone. You can stay there as long as you need to get back to your Lyndheart quest."

"Can I assume the vehicle is hers as well?"

I nodded, trying to keep my eyes on the dusting of snow on the road.

"And where will you go?"

"I... I don't think I should tell you."

He was silent a moment. When I didn't continue, he said, "So that I cannot follow you, correct?"

I swallowed, my mouth turning to cotton. I knew this was going to come up. I didn't want it to. "I... I want my old life back. The ups and downs. All of it. I'm going to see Mark."

"There is something dangerous at Mark's home. Something tied to the Lyndheart." He paused. "And he may very well be dead."

"I... I need to try. I'll be careful. But before I go, I need to apologize to him."

"Why would you apologize?"

"Because I have been with a strange man for weeks now. He deserves an apology." I glanced angry at Edrick. "Because that is how the real-world works."

I could feel more than see the shift in Edrick. It turned the air inside the car dangerous, electric. His face gave no hint of emotion. Yet despite his efforts, his eyes spoke volumes.

We both sat silent for the rest of the car ride. I pulled into the motel. I grew up driving by it my whole life, but never ever in my whole life had any reason to be here. I felt weird pulling in, as if someone would see me and assume things, especially with a man in the car.

Edrick remained in the passenger seat, stewing. His face was neutral, but I could see out of the corner of my right eye his eyes fired up, staring out the windshield. I didn't dare turn to him because I knew I would crumble under that gaze.

"This is the place," I mumbled. Reaching into the coat pocket, I fished out the key with the oversized tag Amy had given me. I trusted her and believed she wouldn't say anything, but a small part of me worried for Edrick. What if someone else said something to the wrong people? Would he be okay?

He's survived hundreds of years without you. What is another night?

119

I forgot I still gripped the key until his hand reached over and snatched it from me. Getting out of the car, he grabbed his sword and the staff. I worried he would ask me to hold onto it. One look at him though, and I knew he wasn't going to waste the words. With the satchel slung over his shoulder, he slammed the door shut. Striding towards one of the rooms, he left tracks in the freshly fallen snow.

Tears began to spill over my eyes as I pulled away from the parking lot and out onto the road. Thankfully, there weren't a whole lot of people out in the snow this late at night. From here, I had a fifteen-minute drive to Mark's. While I should have been watching the snow-covered roads, my brain sped faster than the car the entire way. Free. I had imagined I would be happy, excited. Yet an oppressive weight settled on me. I no longer had the staff, no way to protect myself. I would need to figure out a way to not have to hide my whole life. To not endanger others. But I also needed money. I needed to get a new job. Maybe after I apologized to Mark, I could formulate a better plan.

His house lay a mile ahead. My mind flashed back to the last night I had spoken with him on the phone. The cold, early winter rain had been pouring down. I had been so tired. Work and Mark had been the most stressful things in my life. I had wanted to break up with him. And it felt like the hardest thing to do in the world at the time.

How my life had changed since then.

Did I need to apologize? Did I still want to be with him?

I couldn't even remember how we had met. Barely remembered our time together.

I drove past without slowing down. Where the woman had been killed by the side of the road lay only a fresh coat of snow, no sign of the death or horror from the day before. The lights inside Mark's house were on. And his truck was parked in the driveway. He must finally be home.

I had wanted to see him so badly just hours ago. Did I still want to?

I drove around the block. I just needed another moment to relax. Reaching up for what felt like the hundredth time, I wiped at my nose with my coat sleeve, using the end of the cuff to dry the corners of my eyes, one at a time.

Did I really want to be with him again? Or was I grasping at straws, wanting to go back to everything I had before the monsters, before Edrick, including Mark? The memory of him trying to take care of me after the accident. Him in the hallway, angry that he hadn't been allowed to see me, but Edrick had. Kara, telling me how lucky I was.

I passed his house again, not slowing down. I looked out to the right as I passed. And nearly crashed the car. "You!"

The black-cloaked figure sat in the passenger seat, unmoving. A strange sense of calm settled over me and I somehow knew that it wasn't going to hurt me.

"Yes, I'm real," it finally spoke in a voice that sounded an awful lot like my own, but somehow different. I started to pull over to the side of the road. "No, keep driving."

I paid just enough attention to the road to watch out for cars and road signs, slow enough that the falling and gathering snow on the road wouldn't make the car slip. "Who are you?"

"I'm your naisen vaki," it replied. "You can think of me as the physical embodiment of your life force. I have been with you since before you were born. I have always been with you. In a way, I am you."

"Why are you here?" I asked. It seemed so strange to have a shadow sitting next to me, my exact outline. Talking. At the same time, I could tell I was getting used to strange things just happening. I didn't seem as surprised, shocked, by its presence. "Why have I been able to see you of late? Wait, did you save my life before?"

"Always full of questions. Never calm enough to listen to your own answers," the vaki chided, indicating with a hand void of any light that I should keep my eyes on the road. "I am always with you. And, as of late, I've had to separate myself from you to watch over you," the vaki replied.

"From what?"

"From those of the Chaos Realm who wish to hurt you, to use you for their own means. I cannot tell you everything, Brianna. Part of the reason being, I do not know myself all that is going on. Some of it is because it is more dangerous for you and those around you if you knew everything that was happening. But I have been tasked with keeping an eye on you and keeping you safe."

I gritted my teeth.

The vaki laughed, though the sound seemed... hollow. "No, not him. By the Bai Ze, and that is all I can say of that."

"That sounds familiar." I frowned. "Wait, Bai Ze. Like the book? That thing I found online?"

"I'm sorry. I can't say any more about it."

"You healed me, kept me alive."

"No," the vaki answered. "We aren't sure what that was. Your body had died, but your mind hadn't caught up with it yet," it said, still flat. "Whatever that being had been brought you back and kept you alive until Edrick could get you to the hospital. But to be honest, we still don't know what it was or which side it aligns itself with."

My heart fluttered at the thought of having actually died. "Why did you disappear all those times? If you're me, sent to watch over me, why not just talk to me?"

"I was not allowed to let you know who I am, what I look like. This is not my true form, yet it is the least... distracting."

"So then why show yourself now?" I glanced at the void, devoid of all shapes, shadows, angles, or light. It seemed strange, like nothing existed in the space it occupied. "Why are you just speaking to me now?"

"As I said, I'm not supposed to let you know what I am. But something is happening, something you are at the heart of. I do not know all that is going on and what I do know I cannot reveal other than you are on the threshold of something great and dangerous."

I scoffed. "I'm done with being a Summoner, if you can even consider what little I did being one. I'm going back with Mark—"

"Therein lies the danger," the vaki interrupted. "Clear your mind. Think—"

"I'm done with think—"

"Yeah yeah, I know," it interrupted shortly. "Remember, I've been you longer than you've been you. I know what you've been thinking and feeling. But I also know more. I understand this on a deeper level than you. So," it said, adding a bit of mirth into its flat voice, "shut the fuck up, clear your mind, and focus on Mark. Just him."

I couldn't help but grin and hold back a laugh listening to it. Outside, the snow fell heavier now, flying at the window. Even at thirty miles an hour, it was hypnotic, shrinking the world I knew down to just the vaki and myself within the small confines of the car. "Alright," I conceded. I took a deep breath.

Mark. Mark. Mark.

I felt a slight shudder go up my spine.

"I... don't know if I want to be with Mark."

"You have felt this way for months. Why not?"

I shrugged, turning onto another back road. "It's never felt... great. I mean, he's nice enough. He kinda tries too hard, sometimes. He's pushy, clingy..." I glanced over at the vaki. "I'm always trying to get away from him."

"Now think of Edrick."

Again, I took a slow, deep breath, focusing on the snow outside of the windshield.

Edrick. Edrick. Edrick.

"I already miss him," I whispered, feeling guilty. "I... shouldn't have spoken to him the way I did. He's only ever tried helping me. I'm scared of what can happen around him, yet he has always been there to protect me from everything."

"What has Mark wanted from you?"

"To be his, give him more attention, work less, spend more time with him."

"And Edrick?"

I suddenly felt choked up. I felt like such an asshole. "All he has ever wanted was for me to be able to protect myself, to make sure I stayed safe."

"If you go back to Mark," the vaki began, "you know what will happen. Nothing will change. If you give yourself over to all of his wants, you will become even less. The sense of unease around him will only grow stronger to a point when you cannot leave. There is something wrong about him, something dangerous. I have felt it, just as much as you know you have. I will tell you this, however. Every human has a nasien vaki spirit. Humans are born with them. Mark... I sense that he has none.

"With Edrick, yes, the world seems upside down. He and his kind have spent their lives making sure that you and the rest of the world are exposed to as little of the Chaos Realm as possible. They have given up their childhoods, their lives, for centuries and centuries, merely to protect and defend. They want no thanks, no recognition. You are special. You know, deep down, you can never be free now of the true world around you. Your mind will always feel the tickle of those of us from the Chaos Realm. Without the staff, without training, you will be defenseless from the next attack. And there will be future attacks. Many. Unexpected. Your life can never go back because it has already changed. To try and recapture that will only hurt you and others around you. Even Mark, should you truly wish to go back to him."

"I don't," I said, swallowing past a lump. "I don't want to go back to him."

"Then why would you fight to go back to the past life which is now gone?"

"Because I'm scared," I admitted. "This has all been… too much. Too fast."

"Life is filled with events that happen too fast, with too much force. Accidents. Death. Loss. But also, positive events. Love, celebrations, serendipitous events. It will not be easy, but you must learn to accept and move with all events, both positive and negative. You cannot let the future form around you. You have a power now that almost no one else has. You get to form that future. Happiness and peace will only be found when you learn all you can to protect yourself and others, and not selfishly take and change the world around you just to protect yourself."

Tears were forming again. "Fuck, I'm so sick of crying."

Though there was no face to see, I could imagine the vaki smiling. It felt like Edrick's smile. I laughed, choking on the lump that began to feel like a permanent fixture in my throat.

"I wish I could tell you more," the vaki said softly. "Maybe someday I can. I've already interfered more that I should have. But you are not alone in this world, in this fight, Brianna. There will be others close to you to help you, and who will need your help. But you have to decide now, tonight, which path you will follow, and stick to it. You are out of maneuvers. This last fork in the road will determine your fate and those of all others."

"I don't know if I—"

Out of the corner of my eye, I realized that the vaki had already disappeared. At least visually. I could still feel its presence.

It was me, a part of me. Of course, I could still feel it, it had never left.

Once again, I wiped the tears out of my eyes. Taking several breaths, I turned the car around, and once again headed back towards Mark's house.

CHAPTER 13

I had barely pulled into the driveway when I saw Mark standing at the front door, watching my car enter the driveway. My heart began to beat wildly, but it wasn't the excitement from seeing someone you long missed. I felt a little dizzy, and my stomach twisted in knots. I had always been the one dumped, I had never been the dumper. What would I do if he didn't accept it, if he fought for me to stay with him?

You got this, something deep inside of me coached. I don't know if it was me, or my vaki, which didn't really make a difference I guess since my vaki was me.

Turning off the car, I shoved the keys into my pants pocket. I stepped out into the snowy driveway and made my way up to the house, crossing my arms and shivering a little. My mind buzzed and I felt like I might be sick.

"I see you got a… new car," he started, opening the door for me when I approached close enough.

"Not really," I admitted. "I'm borrowing it."

"From whom?"

"Does it matter?" I snapped as I shut the door behind me.

Mark raised his eyebrows, and I could see a flush creep into his cheeks. He always hated it when I lost my temper or talked back at him. "Sorry, it was just a question. I haven't seen you really in weeks. You're carless, phoneless. I was told you were fired from your job. I've stopped at your apartment a few times. It's been burned to the ground, and I haven't been able to find you." He stepped closer, putting a strong grip on my arm. "I'm just worried about you. I want you to tell me what happened. What's been happening. Where you've been. Who… that guy, is?"

"Look, Mark, we need to talk."

He grabbed my other arm with his other hand, pulling me gently towards him. "I'm sorry if I did anything to hurt you," he began. "I'm just missed you really bad, and I've been extremely worried about you. I just want to make sure that whatever is going on in your life… I can help you. But you need to start talking to me and stop hiding. Here," he said, moving his hands to my shoulders and starting to slide my coat off.

"No, Mark, really, I can't be here long." I wanted to step back and grab the coat from him, but something made me stand still as he took my coat and tossed it over the bench next to the door.

"Why can't you just talk to me?" he pleaded. "That's all I want to do. Talk."

I didn't say anything, I didn't know what to say.

"So…are you okay?"

"I guess," I replied, hesitant.

"Where have you been staying?"

"At my apartment," I replied. "Well, until I got hurt."

"Where did you go after the hospital?"

"I…" *I've been sleeping in old sheds with the guy who has been helping me train to become a Summoner,* came to mind. But I couldn't say that. I had to do everything I could to keep him from growing angry. "I've been staying at friend's houses. Crashing on couches."

"Same friend who lent you the car?"

Here he was, making me mad again with his nosiness. "Yeah."

"Is it a chick or a dude?"

I rolled my eyes. "Jesus Christ, Mark. It's a female friend."

"Okay, well, I just want to make sure—"

"Make sure what? That I'm not hanging out with other guys?" I snapped. "And what if I have been?"

His face grew bright red and dark as he clenched his jaw. "Are you talking about the guy from the hospital? Bob, was it?"

Part of me felt guilty about that. The other part grew angrier. I never got this angry. Was it because of what he was saying? Was it because I finally realized how controlling he was trying to be? "That's none of your business, Mark!"

"I think it would be my business if it has to do with my girlfriend and why she has been acting strange and getting hurt!" He started to yell.

126

I could feel myself growing even more irate. "And so, what if it does have to do with Edrick... I mean, Bob—"

"Edrick." Mark smirked, but it wasn't full of mirth. It was filled with rage.

"Fucking hell. This stops here, now," I muttered. I took a few breaths, holding my fists tight against my side. For some reason, so badly, I wanted to hit him, to choke him. This was the only way to keep me from actually acting out.

Mark took a deep breath, and I could see him physically fighting to shift. "Bri, I'm sorry. You don't deserve me to yell at you. I'm sorry."

I didn't reply, just took a step back.

"Bri, I'm sorry. I love you. "

"I gotta leave," I muttered.

Mark moved closer to me, an intense look to his eyes. "C'mon, Bri. I'm willing to forget whatever happened between that dude and yourself. I just love you. I want to be with you."

I could feel my heart sinking, a dark, heaviness inside of my guts. "Mark, I... I'm sorry..."

"Brianna, don't—"

"...But I, I think we should, well, break up—"

What I had planned in my mind and what spewed from my lips were two different scripts. Before I could finish what I wanted to say, Mark lunged at me. A black, flickering wildness sprang to his eyes. Desperation. I opened my mouth to cry out. His arms reach out and snagged mine. Before I could protest or even react to the suddenness of his assault, he yanked me tight against him. So tight in fact, I felt my chest crushed painfully against his, knocking the wind from me. His lips reached out and covered mine in an aggressive kiss.

No, not a kiss, I thought as I struggled to breathe. His mouth completely covered mine, suffocating. I couldn't even draw a breath from my nose. I don't know what happened other than a horrible sensation invaded every fiber of my being. I wanted to fight back. Instead, my legs buckled, my body collapsed. In seconds that felt like minutes, Mark shoved me away. I tried to stay on my feet, but instead collapsed heavily against the hallway wall, sliding to the floor. His eyes shone dark and massive, absent the whites, glistening with pain and anger. His body trembled slightly, and he wore a wry grin on his face. One that spoke of great, great violence.

"Fine," he hissed. "Go find your mystery man now. Let's see how long before he dumps your ass and I find you crawling back to me." He leaned in as I began sobbing. "Because you *are* mine now, Brianna, and you will come back to me."

A jolt of strength returned as I thrashed my way down the hallway, a horrible, wounded animal sound coming from my throat. My eyes blurred with tears. Yet somehow, I made it out to the car. Somehow, I managed to shove the keys in the damned thing and got it started.

CHAPTER 14

I don't remember much of the drive, which is a horrible thing, considering I could have gotten into yet another accident. Panting, I looked up over the steering wheel and found myself in front of the shabby motel I had put Edrick up in. I didn't know where else to go. Who else to help me. Tears had started drying on my cheeks, in my eyes, leaving my vision blurry. Yet when I looked up and across the nearly empty parking lot, I could see him, peaking from the edge of a worn and thick curtain.

Edrick.

I stumbled from the car, wiping at my eyes, taking deep breaths. I suddenly realized what a train wreck I must have looked. A small part of me didn't care. Not after what I had just been through. I wiped at my face once more, realizing too late what a mess I must have looked. I wrapped my arms across my stomach and shivered. The wind foretold of a coming snowstorm. My eyes glanced down at my trembling arms, and I could see bruises that matched Mark's fingers form across the skin.

Edrick stood at the door and opened it as I reached the threshold. As soon as I stepped inside, he shut and bolted it.

Before he could say anything, and before I even knew what I was doing, I fell against him and started sobbing. I expected him to shove me away after the way I had treated him. Instead, I could feel his familiar slight hesitation before his body relaxed. His arms wrapped themselves gently around me, drawing me into a protective embrace. He said nothing but let me sob into his chest. After some time, I could feel his head resting gently against the top of mine, and his slow, warm, steady breath finally calmed me down.

I have no idea how long I stood there, supported by Edrick's arms. He simply allowed me to cry myself out. But I finally did start to hiccup, and the sobs came to a slow stop. My nose grew stuffy and runny. Aware again of how I must look, I raised one arm and my face away from his sweater so I could wipe at my nose.

Edrick took the movement as an invitation and drew me up tighter against him, just as Mark recently had. Unlike Mark, Edrick held me gently. Even in the state I was in, I could have easily pulled away. I could easily have been the master of my situation. But I was too tired, too hurt, to do anything. Turning my head up, I saw his eyes looking down at me, pinched with concern. I parted my lips to say something, I think to ask for a tissue. I never got the chance.

I could feel his body shift, drawing me in tighter as his head moved closer to mine. I could feel his breath on my skin, and I felt a shudder, but this time not of revulsion.

His lips grazed mine, lingering for a fraction of a second before pressing deeper. My eyes fell shut—

Screams of pain. No, torture. Searing, stabbing sensations, of fire and ice, of every pain I had ever experienced, all at once, and times a hundred.

I could feel us throw each other apart at arm's length. I felt us both falling into separate heaps to the floor. I moaned in agony, the pain slowly subsiding, yet the memory of it all too raw, too fresh.

I opened my eyes and saw Edrick looking at me. Horrified. In pain. Tears had fallen from his eyes and he still groaned, though his eyes stayed wide, unblinking, boring into me.

"What... what the fuck was that?" I finally managed to whimper.

Edrick shakily reached his hand to his lips. I hadn't realized till then, they were raw, and a few drops of blood trickled from what looked like a cut. My lips stung as well. But before I could react, he reached out with his other hand. I felt the tip of one finger gently brush them, but it still hurt. I looked down as he pulled away. A smear of blood, and somehow, in the back of my mind, I knew it wasn't his.

He finally blinked and took a deep breath. Climbing to his feet, he leaned heavily against the door. "I cannot... are you a... no..." He shook his head while he stared at me. I couldn't tell if he was trying to clear it or convince himself of something.

I sniffled, finally wiping my arm across my damp nose. "Edrick, what did you do?"

He continued to shake his head slowly. "No, not what I did. You. But succubi, they cannot... no, you are not, so that leaves..."

His words aggravated the headache forming in my head. "Edrick, please. What... what happened?" I reached out to touch him with a hand.

Edrick jerked back, as if I meant to cause him pain. Just as quickly, I could see he forced himself to hold his arm still, before reaching out and taking my hand. He was scaring me.

"Edrick."

He looked down at my hand on his arm, saw my own bare arm. He quickly reached out with his free hand, grabbing my wrist, not painfully, but not gently either. "Bruises. Fresh."

"Mark he... I mean, I tried to break up with him and he grabbed me..." I shook my head.

"Brianna, you must be honest with me," his somber voice reached my ears. "What did Mark do to you?"

"I went over to break up with him, and he grabbed me. And I..." The memory was already fuzzy feeling. I could see Mark in my mind, I could feel him grab me. "I think I started falling... I don't remember..."

Edrick's face went white. "Brianna, look at me. You must remember. He grabbed you."

I closed my eyes. "He, he grabbed me, and...and..." I could feel a glimpse of it, as if from a long, almost forgotten dream. His mouth pressed against mine, but not in a kiss, and I couldn't move, couldn't breathe.

My other hand had moved up to my mouth, brushing now tender lips.

"Did he kiss you?"

I opened my eyes, feeling my face grow warm with embarrassment. How could I tell him, make him understand? I didn't want Mark to kiss me. Damnit, I was breaking up with him, for good. For Edrick! "It's not what you think—"

"Did he kiss you!" He screamed it, and I jumped.

I couldn't look at him anymore as I nodded. "Yeah, he did. But I—"

"I do not believe it," he whispered. My arm dropped from his grip. I heard the familiar creak of leather and looked up. I hadn't even noticed he was wearing his sword over Mark's jeans, the hem of the sweater covering most of the belt strapped to his waist. I saw his hand wrapped around the grip, white knuckled.

I struggled to take a breath as I scooted myself back, only to find the bed a mere foot away.

Edrick looked down at me. Not the soft, caring man I had come to know, but the man who had first found me. Studying me. Sizing me up, as if I were a target.

"He made me," I whimpered, suddenly fearful of my life. "I was trying to break up with him. I don't want anything to do with him. He grabbed me. He forced himself on me. I—"

Edrick held up his free hand and I fell silent. I don't know what compelled me, but the power radiating off of him made me feel as if I had no option but to obey his every command. He looked down at me a moment longer, huddled on the floor. I didn't want to look at him, but I knew I had no other choice. Finally, his face relaxed. His hand eased off of the grip of his sword. Slowly, his eyes never leaving mine, he knelt in front of me, offering his hand towards me.

I felt like an animal he was trying to coax out of hiding. But I still didn't know his intentions. What had happened between us? I was still too shaken up by the experience. Mark. Everything.

"I will not hurt you," he spoke slowly, softly. "I would never hurt you, Bri." He winced. "Not intentionally."

I looked at him, shocked. "You've never called me Bri."

"There is a first time for everything."

The pain of our lips touching remained too painfully fresh. I wrapped my arms around myself as I looked up at him. I wanted to take his hand, but I didn't think I could. To touch him. What if the pain returned?

Edrick's face took on a pained, vulnerable look. His lips trembled and his eyes began to glisten. "I am sorry I did not see it all before, the signs," he said, still almost in a whisper. "I am sorry I missed the signs."

"What's going on? What is happening to me?"

"Your power, the attraction Dragon has to you. Why he tagged you. How Laura-Lei found you. Possibly why this Shadow Man being is looking for you. Mark's obsession with you. My... attraction... to you. It is not a thing, but a living embodiment. You are the Lyndheart. And Mark knows that."

"The Lyndheart? But how—"

Edrick shook his head. "Mark is not human. He is an incubus, both succubin, but not demon. Children of the dragonfolk. Humans who once gave their lives, their bodies, to the service of dragonfolk so as to avoid death." He lowered his hand. Although he stared at me, his eyes were distant. "Bri, I am so sorry I did not see the signs until now. You and I are now in great danger. They know who you are. Who we both are."

I sniffled. "Edrick, I don't understand."

"I wish you did not have to know at all."

"I don't understand what I'm supposed to know!"

Edrick turned away from me, looking towards the window covered by the curtain. "And now there will be no time to explain. I must leave you. There is something I have to do. Somewhere I must go."

"What? Now?" I stammered. "But where are you going? When will you be back? What about me? What am I supposed to do?"

"I will not be gone long, I hope. I need to find out more information. Dragon knows who you are, knows where we are. And I need to see if any of the other Guardians have encountered information on this Shadow Man. Things have become too perilous to continue without help. I need you to pick up some things for yourself, only essentials. Bare essentials. Then, go into hiding. Speak to and interact with no one. And when I am ready, I will come and find you. And please, do not make any contact with Mark, he is not human. At least, not the human you think you know. He is the most dangerous being to you right now."

"What happened to me? What did Mark do to me?" I began to stand up but felt myself sway. I stood up just enough to sit on the bed. I didn't realize how exhausted I was.

"Mark showed the world who you really are. A danger to everyone. Especially, me. "

I looked up at Edrick and could feel tears in my eyes. I tried to push them down. I didn't want to cry anymore. I wanted answers. I wanted my life to return to before everything. "How am I a danger to you? You have always protected me."

Edrick looked at me. His exhausted expression seemed long, and he looked more haggard than he had ever been. Well, considering I had only known him for a couple weeks now, he looked more haggard than I had ever seen him during that time period. "Because," he said, still staring at me. "My job as a Guardian was to protect the world from the Lyndheart. My job, my life's quest, is to kill you."

I looked at him, in total shock. My heart fluttered painfully. My insides froze. My mind sunk, numb, as if a heavy blanket had smothered my thoughts. All I could hear were his words. *My job is to kill you. My job is to kill you. My job is to kill you.*

He moved faster than I could blink. Edrick stepped in front of me, over me, his eyes boring into mine. I felt the weight of his power. His duty. This was it. I had no powers with me. No weapon. The staff stood across the room, leaning against the wall. Edrick had his hand on his sword, slowly withdrawing it. It hissed and scratched against the wood and leather of the scabbard, a soft, ominous ring as the tip cleared. I swallowed and trembled. I don't think I could have moved if I had even willed it.

My job is to kill you. My job is to kill you. My job is to kill you.

In a single, fluid motion, he dropped the sword tip down heavily into the cheap motel carpet, kneeling behind it. His hands folded on top of each other on the base of the handle, his head bowed lower than his hands. "I have failed in my quest," he said softly. "I may never be forgiven by my brothers for such an offense. However, I know I shall never be capable of completing it. Instead," he brought his eyes up and looked at me once again, "I shall pledge my life, my sword, my duty, to protecting you, at all costs. I will help you find a cure for the incubus curse, and I will find a way to remove the Lyndheart from you without killing you. "

I stared at him, realizing too late that I had my mouth hanging open.

His serious look took on a small, wry grin. "Brianna MacArthur, will you accept me as your sworn protector? And hold me to my oath till my last breath of life?"

"Uh, sure?" I didn't know how to reply. I knew that this occasion was somber and heavy, yet… I was not trained the way Edrick was. Chivalry, oath swearing… none of those things happened anymore in the real world. And even if they did, most people didn't actually uphold them. But I knew he would. Edrick was much, much more different than anyone else I had met.

Edrick… and Mark…

I suddenly shivered as Edrick nodded to me and rose, putting his sword back in its scabbard. "I need to be going. Now. Remember what I said. Pack only essentials. Stay hidden as much as you can. Do not use your name." Grabbing his satchel already sitting by the side of the door, he opened it.

"Wait!" I shouted. "Where am I supposed to go? You never told me how you'll find me, or how long you'll be gone?"

He crossed the room and held my chin in his hand. I flinched, fearing that the pain would return. But there was nothing. Only the strength and warmth of his fingers. "I will find you, Brianna. I will always find you. But… I cannot say how long I will be gone for. Not long. I have to get more information, and I cannot do that from here." I could see he fought himself to lean in and kiss me. Instead, his hand fell to behind my back, pulling me close against him. He held me for a few seconds before letting go. I realized, too late, I should have held him back. Told him not to go.

Without another word, Edrick walked out and shut the door. I sat, dumbstruck, on the bed. When I finally managed to get up, exhausted, feeling as if I weighed a million pounds, I looked out the window. Looking for him. The snowflakes drifted lazily down, catching the lights from nearby buildings, and passing cars. A million specks of firelight. Yet it had snowed enough in those few minutes to hide any tracks Edrick left. I didn't even know in which direction he had gone. Turning my eyes back inside the room, I could have fooled myself that he had never even been there. That he wasn't real. That everything that had happened the past few weeks hadn't actually happened at all

Yet the thin, dingy carpet said otherwise. A single spot, as if something heavy, profound, had forced its way in the threads, leaving the smallest of holes. No one else would ever see it. But I saw it with startling clarity.

It was all real.

Made in the USA
Middletown, DE
01 May 2021